Leave to Remain

To ~~Dearest~~ Naomi,

With much love and respect

Suzi

London, May 2008

Visit www.booksurge.com to order additional copies.

Cover image: Getty Images/Guliver Image Croatia
Cover design: Cameron Moyer

Leave to Remain

S.D. Curtis

2007

1

He can guess that she is as old as he is by the tiny lines which are starting to gather in the corners of her eyes. Perhaps even she hasn't noticed them yet; convinced by the youth that she has possessed all her life.

'Name?'

He hands through the receipt they gave him on his last visit, on which his surname and the date of application are printed.

She glances down at the paper, then turns to an open drawer at her side and begins to slide forward the files as she searches for a match.

'Christian name?' she asks without looking up at him, her fingers poised inside a yellow folder.

'I am not a Christian.'

She turns to him now and looks him up and down with an efficient flick of her eyes.

'I believe this is your file,' she continues, with a slight lilt in her voice to show that she has chosen to ignore his comment. She takes the folder out of the drawer and opens it on the desk in front of her.

'I am afraid that your application for a visa has been rejected.'

'For what reason?'

"We cannot accept an application without the necessary documentation."

She passes his forms back under the glass screen towards his hands which are resting on the other side.

"But I put in all the things that were listed in the guidelines."

He says 'things': he means documents, letters of reference, proof of status, but his English fails him. He has remembered 'guidelines' though - she must give him credit for that.

"I am sorry, Mr....' she looks down for the forgotten name but it has already gone back to him under the glass, 'but we require a guarantee letter from a person or a company who is willing to sponsor you during your stay.'

'But it didn't say so in your forms...your guidelines'

'It is an extra requirement for citizens of certain countries, if you read our website...'

'I don't have a computer' he interrupts her, cutting off her assumptions before she has time to take them too far.

'Well, I'm sorry but those are the requirements.'

Her eyes have barely registered his face and already they are searching beyond his shoulders for the person who is waiting behind him.

'You must put all you want me to do on paper,' his finger stubs the counter and the pile of forms which have been returned to him. 'It wasn't in the rules. I don't know anybody in your country can give me guarantee letter.'

'I am sorry sir but there is nothing I can do for you without the necessary documentation.'

'Next time you have to tell me everything what I need to do. And if I need to fuck the ambassador's wife to get a visa, then you have to put it in the guidelines.'

His tone does not rise and at first she doesn't register what he has said. Then her lips tighten and she makes as if to turn towards the door to her left; behind which there lies all the certainty and power of her country.

But he has already walked away and the next face is waiting behind the glass: wad of papers expectantly thrust forward, ready to pass under the counter.

***

Out on the street it is cold and damp. There is a north wind today and the last dry leaves are being blown from their branches onto the tarmac. His hand moves up instinctively to the edges of his eyes, where he feels the same small indentations on his own rough skin.

Out of habit he looks at his watch and calculates that he has wasted three hours queuing and waiting for another rejection. Around him there are still people on the pavement who haven't yet been let into the building. He knows from experience that it is now too late for them to be given a chance to get near the woman he has just spoken to. Perhaps they also know it but still they wait in the hope that today the line will move faster or that for once the embassy staff will be lax and go past the eleven o'clock deadline.

He nods in recognition at one of the faces which turn to him with a smile; a middle-aged woman whose features so closely resemble so many other middle-aged women from his country that he cannot identify where he knows her from. 'Good luck,' he tells her, not in their own tongue but in Lithuanian, the language of the country where they now both find themselves. It is a private joke between them all; the irony of the fact that 'luck' in Lithuanian sounds like the word 'pity' in their language.

Walking quickly now, he moves like an intruder through the unfamiliar quarter of Vilnius' old town. Usually, he has no business to move around these pristinely refurbished streets; amongst the new clothing stores and leather shops, the boutiques offering brightly coloured ceramics and amber jewellery to the more inquisitive tourists who venture into the increasingly popular Baltic Republics. Enclosed like a pearl between the Vilnia and Neris rivers, this is the reserve of foreigners and the nouveau riche of a confident, new generation. The part of the city where the refugee centre is located is the home of the old order: of potholed roads and pavements, rusty railings bent from years of hard winters, cheap Russian shops selling vodka or brandy, and the all pervasive aura of neglect.

He crosses the road, weaving between the lines of pristine cars which are parked neatly along both sides. Back home, his uncle had given him his old car after his wife had her second child. It was an ancient Fiat - two doors, no air conditioning for comfort or air bag for safety. He had parked it in the garage of his maternal aunt and left her one of the keys, despite the fact that she couldn't drive. The other key he still keeps in a compartment of his wallet, although the garage is no longer there and the car was buried along with the body of his aunt under the bombed ruins of what was once a four-story building. She had lived on the first floor: no chance of escaping that weight.

On the corner of the long straight swathe of Gedimino Prospect he finds his bicycle where he left it; chained to a metal fence protecting a cluster of vulnerable saplings. There is something satisfying to him about the precise geometry of this road – slicing through the city form east to west; from the shabby nineteenth century apartments to the calm white columns of the Neo-Classical cathedral. He was told by a bitter Russian resident that it used to be called Lenin Prospect, before the Lithuanians gained independence and renamed it after the legendary founder of their beloved city.

4

Bending, he opens the bicycle lock with another key that he keeps in the small upper pocket of his jeans along with the key of his suitcase. These are the only three keys that he possesses now: there is no lock on his communal room, no front door in the place where he lives. His bicycle is his most expensive possession and he treats it very carefully. There is no excess oil on the chain to spoil his trousers, no rust on the spokes. It was a present from his mother's cousin – his only living relative in the country. As a boy he would spend every summer with her, in the farm which she and her Lithuanian husband kept before they moved to Vilnius. Back then, her husband found a kind of satisfaction in allowing a poor cousin from a distant and neglected corner of the USSR to indulge in the privileges of his homeland. But when he came to them as a refugee the hospitality was quickly withdrawn: even family have limits.

He has to cycle very carefully for they are not accustomed to cyclists in this city. He pedals very slowly, letting the motion of the tires tick over just enough to stop him from falling off. The streets are clean and well maintained; there are no unsightly potholes or rubbish clogging the curb sides. In any other situation, he would find this pleasing, but now it only angers him. When there are not too many pedestrians, he mounts the pavement and overtakes the queuing traffic. As he rides he tries to avoid spoiling his newly laundered trousers against the filthy metal; for in the build-up to the long, grey winters the cars are already gathering their protective layer of dust and grime. By November they will be thickly encased in a coat of dirt which will see them through the frost and the snow until the spring comes and their owners feel it is worth the effort to wash them again.

Waiting at the traffic lights, a voice calls to him from the opposite pavement and he turns to see a hand rise up above the heads from a café on the opposite corner. A group of boys from the centre have occupied one of the tables arranged on the pavement, taking advantage of the last vestiges of the pale autumn sun. He changes directions and manoeuvres the bike between the lanes of traffic, then dismounts and bends down to lock it.

'Who do you reckon is going to steal it, Azad?' laughs one of boys seated at the table.

'You never know!' Azad rejoins, putting the key carefully back in his jeans pocket. He notices that the others are all younger him by at least eight years, making them still teenagers, and instinctively his hands moves gently across his prematurely thinning hairline. Most of the other males in the centre are either older or younger than him; he is almost unique of his generation and he knows very well that he should either be back home fighting or somewhere else making money.

He sits down and raises his hand to call for the waiter (theirs may never have been a rich society but there was always enough time and money to sit and drink with friends at a café). Looking around the table he nods to each familiar face in turn.

'As sala'amu alaikum,' one of them intones, his voice a little too loud, but Azad does not react; still uneasy with these shows of religion that have suddenly become a marker for patriotism.

'Aren't you supposed to be at school?' he asks in retaliation.

'We don't have to be there until two - they won't let us in until theirs have finished.'

He knows very well that at home they would have long finished high school but the war has put everything on hold. As they are allowed to remain in Lithuania only at the goodwill of the government, they must abide by the conditions which they decide: only when all the regular pupils and teachers have gone home can the refugee children use the classrooms to receive lessons from the few educated men and women among them who are willing to teach voluntarily.

The waiter arrives and leans across him to put a cup of coffee onto the table and to tuck the bill neatly under the ashtray where there are already two waiting. He takes them immediately and pays for everything: it is another duty of the eldest male and the others don't even notice the gesture.

When they have finished drinking, he finds himself alone with Benjamin, the youngest of the group (like the Old Testament story, he thinks to himself: wasn't he the one who finally moved Joseph's conscience not to take revenge on his brothers?).
'How's your family?' Azad asks, automatically. It is the obligatory and the expected question, yet it is not such a simple thing to ask, for in these circumstances there is every chance that they may no longer be alive: so etiquette is made an act of courage.
'They're fine, Thank God.' Benjamin adds the last two words like one adds 'please' to a request. His light blue eyes, so unusual in his country, flit briefly into the distance and then return again. Then he laughs unexpectedly and reaches into his bag under the table. Pulling out a clear jar full of honey, he unscrews the lid and takes a spoon from one of the coffee cups to scoop some out.
'My grandfather sent it to me from home, can you believe it? He got some journalist to smuggle it out to Moscow and then my cousin brought it here by bus.'
The both of them laugh and Benjamin's broad smile opens to let in the golden substance while Azad watches him with amusement. There is something about Benjamin's untarnished joy for life which he finds fascinating.
'It's good stuff I bet, your grandfather must know what he's doing.'

7

'He's eighty-six and still fit as a fiddle and he swears it's due to a spoon-full of this every morning.'

'My uncle produces the best honey in the region - and the best sour cream.'

'You want to discuss with my grandfather about that?' Benjamin retorts.

Azad takes a spoon from his own cup and leans over towards Benjamin in order to take some of the honey from the still-open jar. It is sweet and thick, slipping slowly down his throat. Benjamin screws the lid back on and indicates to the building across the street.

'Have you heard who got a job at McDonald's? - Stony, I saw him there yesterday.'

Almost every male in the refugee centre has a nickname and most of the time nobody ever bothers to learn their real one. Stony has been so named because he smiles so rarely. Unlike most teenagers in the refugee centre, his parents did not send him on to safety while they stayed behind to protect the family home. Stony's parents went on to Germany, where they now have residency, and no one has ever dared to ask him why he didn't join them.

'How did he manage that, without a work permit?' Azad asks, his pride piqued by the remembrance of his own lack of work.

'Bribed some local guy to lend him his National Insurance number, apparently.'

'And the language? I don't remember Stony as a great linguist.'

Benjamin laughs, 'he only had to learn a few phrases off by heart. The manager knows, of course, but what does he care as long as he gets the workers?'

Azad nods silently at the wholesome logic.

'Let's go and say hello!' Benjamin adds mischievously and scrapes his chair along the tarmac as he gets up to leave. The two of them walk across the street, leaving the bicycle parked against the wall.

Inside the sparkling glass wall of McDonalds, the colours are all familiar. He knows that this is deliberate: that the owners of this chain want people to be able to step off any unfamiliar street, anywhere in the world and feel that they have come, in a sense, back home. But the two of them do not come from a world where there are McDonalds in every town. For him, this place looks like a backdrop to a scene in an American film. Yet despite himself, he is almost caught up in the fantasy that he is somewhere else, that he is free and successful and that life is full of a whole variety of possibilities which he can choose according to his heart's desire.

'I heard that when they opened this place a priest came to bless it with Holy Water. They didn't come to the refugee centre but they came to McDonalds.'
Azad's voice is sharp with unconcealed animosity, but Benjamin shrugs his shoulders in response,
'Perhaps they didn't think it appropriate, what with most of the refugees being Muslim.'
'What difference does that make? You think that Muslims aren't allowed in McDonalds, or that this is some kind of Christian place?'
Benjamin jerks his head to the side as if to dismiss the argument, 'Do you think that the food here is any better than in the centre, though?'
The two of them laugh, and over the heads of the queuing customers Benjamin waves to his friend serving at the counter. Stony winks in return and makes a movement with his eyes to indicate that they should queue up too.
'Last time we got free milkshakes,' Benjamin explains, and the two of them add themselves to the line.

9

The place is full of light and chatter. And excess: there are too many people in the small foyer space, not enough chairs to accommodate all the diners, not enough bins to contain all the discarded paper cups and polystyrene containers. When they reach Stony, he gives them two large cokes with ice and they pass over a couple of small coins, which he hastily rings into the till.

'Like the hat!' Benjamin jokes.

'They pay seven Euros an hour. I'd walk around bare-assed for that.'

Stony maintains the blank expression he is known for as he says this and it is only Benjamin that laughs.

2

Outside all is dark but not quite still. He can hear the rats scuttling to and fro: rummaging in the bins and nibbling at scraps of food. He does not know where rats usually make their homes; under buildings, in the gaps and spaces which are left unseen when the whole structure is built. This building must have a lot of rats, for it is full of forgotten holes and concealed corners. Every room is stuffed with bags and suitcases, piles of books and packets of dried foods, behind which a whole army of rodents could make their own secret city; living out their life in parallel to the humans that inhabit the world above them. Yet in the daytime it is a silent city; for it is only at night that their existence becomes audible.

He turns over onto his left side and hears the person to his right echo the movement in his sleep. There is also another man sleeping by the door, but he is too far away to be disturbed. The beds that they have been given are too narrow and the mattresses are thin, so that after a while his ribs begin to ache and he is forced to turn over. He has managed to acquire an extra blanket from the Red Cross store and has folded it carefully under the sheets but it only delays the reaction. Turning, he is forced to face his roommate, which will make it even harder to fall asleep. Laying in the dark together, he becomes obsessed by the other man's breathing until it seems so loud that it forces him to follow the imposed rhythm.

He knows that tomorrow is an important day for him and that he must be prepared for it, but the more he thinks of this the further sleep recedes from him. Since his arrival here, rest of any sort has become a slippery and unreliable commodity: much sought after and rarely satisfactory. They gave him sleeping pills at the clinic, but they only leave him groggy and nauseous. He only sleeps well when he has been out drinking or on the rare occasion that he has brought back a woman and they have slept together on the hard mattress.

He leans across to the bedside cabinet that separates his bed from the other man's and picks up his wristwatch. If he holds it at a certain angle he can just make out the luminescence of the dial: it is two thirty. When he cannot sleep like this, he imagines it is because there is someone thinking of him; not allowing him to sleep by the sheer force of their thoughts. In his mind he can identify two possibilities: his mother and the woman he used to call his girlfriend. He allows himself to think about his mother as often as he has the possibility to call her; most weeks he manages at least once. As for the other woman, he will not indulge his mind's insistence on recalling her. He keeps his mind closed so tight that he can hardly make his way through to where his memories of her are caught. Behind the mess of fear and guilt is the place where she still exists for him and it is only occasionally at night, when his defences are sagging from the day's struggle, that he sometimes lets her in.

And she is here now: the particular smell of her skin, the two lines between her eyebrows contracted together in concentration even in her sleep. His uncle had warned him, 'that girl thinks too much, one day she'll out-think the two of you'. It was half machismo of course, but also half truth. Unlike the rest of his friends, she hadn't ignored the growing signs of tension which would slowly and inevitably lead to war. While the rest of the population laughed at the idea of an armed conflict, she was attending meetings with a whole different set of people: the kind who sense danger like animals sense movement or the changing of the weather. She began to talk of acquiring weapons, of the need to be prepared to fight for a just government based on the laws of Islam. But her words were like quotations from foreign songs to people who had been brought up on the Soviet propaganda of secular camaraderie.

In the end, her prophesies came true. Protests were organised and speeches were read calling for an end to the oppressive regime. Half the people came in the name of revolution, while the rest came out of simple desperation at the growing prices and increasing poverty. Neither of them attended: he through apathy and disbelief and she through the conviction that the time for talking was over. By that point her disgust with her own people had extended even to him. The protests were reported in the press as dangerous riots orchestrated by the radical Islamicists and the army were sent from the capital. Out of the tranquil hills came the gunfire that wasn't to stop for the next two years.

Sleep is coming now and in between the shifts in consciousness he is acutely aware of an excruciating sense of nostalgia which comes from somewhere in his chest and seems to sink inside him like a lead weight.

***

He is woken by the soft click of the door as it's pulled closed behind someone leaving. Raising his head slightly off the mattress, he looks over to the bed opposite to find only a mess of discarded sheets and blankets. Pulling himself up onto one elbow, he can make out the time on his watch and the figure of his second roommate, Ismail, already awake and propped up on two pillows reading the newspaper. He is annoyed that he is not alone to be able to make the trip to the communal bathroom without the discomfort of eyes upon him.

Standing up in the white underpants which are standard Red Cross issue, he puts on a jumper over his bare chest and pulls on his jeans. Then he slides his feet into the slippers that he places neatly by his bed every night and goes out into the corridor. Ismail doesn't visibly look up from his papers, following the un-written rule between the two of them not to communicate unless absolutely necessary. Ismail is one of those who have developed new-found fervour in his religion since the Russian rule collapsed. He is inspired by those who give up their life in a martyrdom of fire and bloodshed, and among some people in the centre he is a visionary. Forced to share a room together, they both quickly understood that the only workable agreement between them was the compromise of silence.

The bathroom floors are covered with vinyl which has been cut badly and curls up around the doorposts, making the cubicle doors difficult to close. He pushes his weight against the handle until he can hear it slot into place, then pulls the wire tight over the nail in order to lock it. For once, there is no movement in the adjacent cabin and he almost relaxes as he feels the hot water hit his back. He takes the liquid soap into his hands and works on himself until he feels relief well up inside him and spill out onto the grubby white enamel. Almost immediately afterwards, he can hear the main door of the bathroom opening and the movement of hands as someone takes off their clothes and hangs them on the chair, before turning on the water in the shower next to him.

When he comes back from the bathroom, Ismail is not there. He notices his dirty shoes still under the bed and realises that it must have been him who entered the shower next to his. Feeling a sudden urge to leave before he returns, he hangs up his towel to dry on the windowsill and quickly pulls on his shirt and trousers. It is still early but he wants to have a coffee in town before his appointment. Today is the day when he will finally get to meet the Dean of Vilnius Technical University. It is part of his two pronged attack to continue to apply for visas to get him out of Lithuania, while at the same time trying to improve his situation here. As he is fond of saying, he has no time to waste on hope or prayer to improve his life. The technical university is the only one which has so far been willing to admit refugee students onto their courses and he is only the third one to be granted an interview. As his people have not been given full refugee status by the government, schooling and medical care are not theirs by right but favours to be bestowed on an individual basis.

He takes a thin, cardboard file of photocopies from his bedside table: he knows it is not enough, nowhere near enough proof of the four years he had passed at his home university. He has no record sheet of seminars attended neatly signed by the professor in the narrow right-hand columns; no exam score sheets with the official stamp of the faculty. All he has, in fact, are a few photocopies of class registers and the letter he received on his twenty-first birthday admitting him onto a course of Mechanical Engineering. These documents were somehow resurrected and acquired by the determined patience of his mother- a woman who left school at the age of fourteen and was married at sixteen. He places them carefully now in his rucksack. As he passes through the door, he narrowly avoids the shoulder of his returning roommate.

It is still early morning and outside many of the refugees have simply thrown a coat or a sweater over their bedclothes in order to make the short walk to the kitchen, where they each receive the entitled breakfast allowance of two pieces of white bread and two sachets of marmalade. Some of them are carrying the sweet tea which is served in enamel cups but most prefer to boil coffee in their rooms on electric rings which they have installed illegally. His room, with three young men inside, does not contain such an appliance but he is well supplied with hot coffee by the numerous old women who inhabit his barrack and who take it as their duty to look after the single males. Today he has left on an empty stomach; he tells himself that this is so he can keep a clear head for his interview, although deep down he knows that he is too nervous to eat. He is fully aware that his future may well rest on the ten minutes in which he will be allowed to state his case.

He crosses the forecourt which separates 'B' barrack from the 'A' barrack where he lives, walking past the guard box and out of the gate. The barracks and the concrete pitch around them once housed a Soviet military unit, and he can see the irony in the fact that the refugees have been forced to flee their country because of Russian-made bombs and weapons, and yet have found shelter in their old headquarters. The entire complex is surrounded by a two-meter wire mesh fence which he must walk around before reaching the gravel path which leads to the terminus of the one city bus that serves this neglected suburb.

Curious faces peer out at him from parted curtains as he passes by and he feels suddenly self-conscious in his best trousers and corduroy jacket. Because he does not work in the market or as a labourer for one of the many building firms, he knows he has a reputation as an 'intellectual': he is an urban man in the midst of rural people, a rare product of the city who did not have the international contacts or the money to afford private accommodation. Yet he takes a perverse pride in his situation; in the exaggerated scenario that he has stuck with the common people rather than pursuing the preservation of status. He would like them to say of him, 'he was a man of the people'; but he knows that he must go a long way before he can live up to that.

When he reaches the bus stop, the vehicle is waiting with its engines running. He fingers the ticket he has carefully put in his jacket pocket and hesitates before validating it in the small, orange box which is attached to one of the hand-rails. Normally, he would risk the appearance of a controller and try to bluff his way out by claiming he didn't understand the validation system but today he doesn't want to risk the delay it would inevitably cause. The controllers are used to the tricks which the refugees use in order to avoid the fare and although they have no real way of forcing a fine on someone with no fixed address, they like to exercise their authority by insisting on trips to the police station and the filling-in of endless forms.

The bus rumbles slowly through the seemingly endless suburbs of car warehouses, garages and shabby housing which typify the outskirts of the city. Eventually, it passes the railways tracks and shunts towards the long swathe of Pylimo Avenue, which wraps itself around the border of the old town with grey functionality. Despite himself, his eyes are drawn once again to the heavy mass of the old city wall and the loose bundle of beggars and invalids which always congregate around the archway. He has glimpsed the interior of the church which they come to pray at: the baroque extravagance of burnished gold and marble, the pious features of saints robed in blues and reds. To him these grotesque renditions of human piety are simultaneously horrifying and fascinating. Recklessly, his mind would recall the clean lines and geometric patterns of the mosques back home: turquoise domes; shadows draping themselves across the sand-coloured stone; but he erases these images as quickly as they arrive, roping in his melancholic longing for the shapes and colours of a place he has left behind.

He arrives at the solid stone edifice of the technical university exactly five minutes before his interview is scheduled: prompt yet keen not to appear too desperate. Outside on the grey, granite steps he must walk past the clusters of teenagers who have gathered to gossip and smoke, but they pay no attention to him. Perhaps, given the age difference, they take him for an assistant professor.

The secretary, positioned like a guard outside the dean's office, is in her mid-fifties but trying hard not to be. Her face has a slight orange glow from the excess of make-up and her shoulders rise in defence when she realises that he is walking towards her. Silently, he hands her the letter of invitation from the Admissions Officer, unwilling to risk compromising himself in front of her by mispronouncing a word in her language.

Without even a hint of a smile, she tells him to sit down and wait and he lowers himself into one of the red plastic chairs that have been placed on either side of the door. He can feel her eyes watching him as he fingers the already well-thumbed file that rests on his knees. Shuffling his weight so that he can lean back almost comfortably in the chair, he prepares himself for a long wait: he has become accustomed to being at the end of people's lists of priorities.

After forty minutes, the secretary looks up briskly from her papers and tells him he can enter. Inside, he finds himself in front of a wide oblong desk, behind which there sits a small man with greying hair and the stained moustache of a life-long smoker. The dean gestures casually towards the chair on the other side of his desk, and Azad lowers himself once again into the red plastic, resting the precious file on the table between them.

'I received your application to study at the Mechanical Engineering Department,' the dean coughs and shuffles the pile of papers stacked on his left-hand side, until he has found the one he is looking for. 'Did you manage to bring any documentation from your home university?'

'I have brought these papers,'

The dean takes the pale, beige file from his outstretched hands and opens it slowly. Like someone accustomed to their own authority, he does not hurry through what he finds there but lifts up each page to examine its contents before placing it face-down on the open cover and continuing to the next one.

'You have no formal records of your studies?' he asks finally, without lifting his gaze from his desk.

'Only what you have there.'

'Attendance sheets, exam results?'

'You see,' Azad begins, then hesitates, for there is a provocative and a neutral way to reply and he must not let the one slip into the other, 'the faculty where I went was bombed just after I came here. Almost all records were destroyed in the fire.'

The dean looks up from his papers at this reply but his face still retains its look of superior neutrality.

'And this is all the documentation you brought with you?'

'No, this is the result of all my mother's asking and begging for the last few months.'

He knows he risks sounding insolent with this but his knowledge of the language doesn't allow for subtleties.

The dean nods, as if in appreciation of the commitment of this woman whom he can only barely imagine.

'You speak Lithuanian well.'

'I used to come here as a child – I picked it up from the other kids,' he pauses, then adds, 'and I've had the chance to practice over the past twelve months.'

The dean lets his eyes linger over the face of Azad for a fraction of a second longer than normal, as if he is trying to penetrate behind those impassive features to the place where vulnerability and humanity lie. Then takes a pen from his desk and makes a note on the papers in front of him. Despite his apparent indifference, there is sympathy deep inside him for these people who have been so brutally forced to seek refuge in his country, born of his own memories of grandparents uprooted by the Second World War.

'You will have to sit the end of year exam for the second year in order to enter the third. If you succeed, you can start in three weeks when classes begin.'

'But I had almost finished my forth year.'

'In another country and another language.' He closes the file on his desk and gives the weakest of smiles by way of compensation. He knows very well that he is doing more than most of his colleagues ever would.

'You must come on Monday to collect the letter which I will leave with my secretary and take it to the Head of Department. He will let you have the list of texts to study for the exam,' he pauses to hand back the file across the desk, 'I will warn him of your coming.'

***

Inside the club there are only a few people whom he knows. It is not the usual day for the other refugees from his centre; they prefer the anonymity of Saturday night crowds. On the dance floor he recognises Benjamin's girlfriend, out for once without him and laughing with a group of other girls (they are probably foreigners like herself, he assumes from their paleness - perhaps teachers from the same school). He has met her once or twice before but never spoken directly to her. He knows very well how proud Benjamin is of her: like he is proud of the Levi jeans some distant cousin sent him from America and the fact that he can speak English better than any of his peers.

Her hair is a pale blond, cut very precisely at the nape of her neck and her features are small and unobtrusive in themselves, yet as a whole they have a neat perfection. Captivated, he watches the way she moves her body to the beat of the songs, with an expression which isn't quite a smile but seems to come from some inner satisfaction with what she is doing at that moment.

She has stopped dancing now and as she moves to lean against the wall she catches his eye and smiles in recognition. He walks over to her and offers the half-empty glass of beer he is holding and she takes it and smiles self-consciously before drinking it down in one swig.

He can see her better close-to: her skin is fine, almost translucent, there are beads of perspiration on her forehead and her make-up has smudged beneath her eyes. He is aware of pity moving inside him like an insect crawling through the earth and all at once he feels both repelled and fascinated.
'You enjoying?' he asks: his English broken but confident.
'The dancing or the music?'
'Both.'
'Not the music really but it feels good to dance. I don't do much exercise otherwise,' she laughs self-consciously.
He looks her up and down, 'You don't need.'
She smiles briefly and makes a dismissive gesture with her hand, then looks behind her at the dancers still on the floor so as to avoid his stare. She knows him by sight only, from Benjamin's group of friends and she has seen him a couple of times around town: his dark, sharp figure so conspicuous amongst the pale skins of the Lithuanians. There is something about the way he holds himself which intrigues her – as if his whole body were being blown by the force of a strong wind; his muscles in

constant tension against the blast of an invisible force which tries, but never manages, to topple him over.

Out of the crowd another girl comes over and stands beside her; she is still breathing heavily from dancing and has to wait a few moments before speaking.
'Do you want a drink, Lucy?' she asks, when she has regained her breath.
"I'll have a beer, thanks.'
The friend searches on the ground against the wall for her bag and as she bends he notices a bulge of white flesh buckle between her trousers and her short shirt. When she retrieves her purse she looks back at Lucy and then over at him. He can tell that she is taking in his dark hair and skin, trying to make him fit into one of the categories which she has carefully filed into her mind.
'What about you?'
'A beer, if you're offering.'
'And if I wasn't?' she retorts, but he doesn't catch her meaning and remains silent. He is thinking about the name Lucy and cannot imagine how he could not have known it before. Is it possible that Benjamin had always referred to her simply as 'my girlfriend'?
The girl moves away, leaving the two of them alone again.
'Do you live…?' Lucy hesitates, as if remembering a secret that she isn't supposed to give away, '…with Benjamin?'
'In the refugee centre, you mean?'
He never fails to exploit someone's shyness about his situation; it is one of the few feelings of power he has access to.
She nods and smiles, unable to tell from his face if he is offended.
'We both live in the same barrack,' he adds, not willing to let the moment go just yet. She shifts her weight uncomfortably.
'You?' he adds.

'I live with Emma,' she gestures to where the other girl is standing by the bar. 'We have a small flat, one-bedroom, by the Vilnia river.'

'Nice.'

'It's ok, a bit squashed. It's rented by the language school - we get it as part of our contract.'

'It's better that way. If they hear you are foreigners they would charge double for an apartment here.'

His manner is suddenly neutral, as if there is no difference between the two of them.

'I can imagine, I always get charged more for taxi rides as well.'

There is almost a gratefulness in her tone as she replies, as if this is the first time that anyone other than Benjamin has taken her as a person and not a foreigner.

Emma returns with the drinks and hands them both their beers.

'You drink alcohol, then?' she asks him.

'Emma!' Lucy interrupts, but her voice collides with his.

'We are modern Muslims, you know.'

His tone is condescending and she rises to meet it.

'But I thought that Muslims weren't allowed alcohol?'

He is quick to answer; he has done this so many times before,

'And I think that in your religion you should eat fish on Friday and not have sex before marriage, is it not so?'

'I'm not practising.'

'Why do you think I am?'

Emma doesn't answer him but shrugs her shoulders and turns back to Lucy.

'I'm going to dance, watch my bag,' she commands.

The two of them watch her push her way into the crowd until she is lost from view.

'We don't cut up our women either,' he says, his voice so low she can hardly catch it.

She looks at him in the eyes for the first time. They are a very pale green with a light brown rim and the flesh around them seems almost bruised by what she guesses is tiredness.

'I know that,' she answers softly.

Simultaneously, they look away towards the dance floor and for a few minutes neither of them speaks.

'Do you manage to speak to your family often?'

She ventures out heedlessly onto the thin ice of uncharted suffering, as if they have already known each other for a long time.

'I call my mother one time in a week, if it is possible. She tells me about the others – her sisters, my uncles and cousins.'

'Where do you come from?'

He laughs briefly at the vast gap in understanding which will inevitably open between the quaint enquiry and the inadequacy of his answer,

'If you translate the name exactly, it means City of Almonds.'

'Sounds beautiful.'

'It is at the centre of the war – the whole valley is... I can say...very dangerous.'

He watches her face pale slightly, and she does not reply for some time.

'I try to follow it on the TV but it's not always easy for outsiders to understand what's going on,' she blurts out finally, 'do you know what I mean?'

'People in the West only understand national borders, they like *categories*,' he pronounces the word slowly, as if testing it out for the first time. 'For seventy years we were under the Russians – then we were communists, now we are Muslims. The fighting is not just about religion. It is about power, money, revenge....and it goes across all borders.'

She hesitates before replying, but he looks at her so intently that she is almost compelled to defend herself,

'There is so much fear of terrorism…any sign of fundamentalism in a country which is so near Afghanistan sends out warning signals to the Americans.'

He laughs without humour, 'It is not so simple like they want to show – Muslim fundamentalists against pro-democratic forces. The Americans always believe the governments who shout about democracy and anti-terrorism, but many times it is the army and the police who act like criminals – they arrest and torture people with no reason. And so the people turn to Islam because they think it will give them back some order, some morals.'

'The Americans are afraid that the Muslims want to set up a caliphate stretching right across Central Asia.'

He looks at her with a spark of anger beginning to ignite in his pale eyes.

'Do we look like fundamentalists? What I know is that all ordinary people want is a safe country where they can have an honest life and don't have to hide from the police.'

She looks away, shy in face of his anger, and he relinquishes a little.

'It is strange for me too – all this talk of Islam after all these years. But there is so much unhappiness, so much fear. Under the Russians everyone had work and bread, and nobody think about religion. I don't know what will come of all this.'

They both reach for their drinks at the same time and the conversation is interrupted. He takes his cigarettes from his pocket and offers her one. When she leans forward to light it, he notices the fine line of her neck and shoulders.

'You do not miss your home?'

The question makes her uncomfortable; she has heard it so many times from Benjamin's friends. Normally, she would say that she missed her parents and her brothers, but that she came here for work: they all understand the idea of economic migration. But there is something about him which doesn't allow her to pretend.

'There is a vast difference from leaving of your own free will and being forced out. I can go back whenever I want, so I don't feel the urgency.'

'Why Vilnius? I have to be here but you don't.'

She looks at his eyes and realises he is teasing, 'My mom's parents come from here originally, they moved to the States during the Second World War. I came here with them once on holiday when I was a kid and then when I left college, it seemed like a good idea to spend some time here - get to know my roots.'

He looks at her quizzically and she senses that he is unconvinced by her words.

'I like it here, really: the old town, the fact that you can get into the countryside so easily. It's so small and safe.'

'Safe,' he repeats, as if he doesn't understand the word.

'It may sound strange to you but America isn't all like it is on the films – expensive cars and big houses and families with perfect teeth. There's a lot of poverty, a lot of crime.'

'It is not strange. I also come here to be safe.'

Out on the dance floor there is a change in tempo, and they are caught up for a brief moment in a crowd exiting towards the bar. Forced by the swell to move aside, they retreat together to the far wall.

'You want to stay?' he asks, when she has turned back to him.

'Not particularly.'

'We can go for coffee.'

It is a question, although he says it like a statement.

She looks at him without answering; trying to work out what lies behind his words; but he never gives anything away by his expression. Then she nods and follows him through the tight throng of bodies to the door, where she stops to take her coat from the cloakroom. When she comes out into the night she finds him waiting outside smoking a cigarette. Unintentionally, she notices that he holds it in that inverted way that some men have, almost cupping the lighted end in his palm.

When he sees her exit he flicks the butt from his hand, leaving it glowing on the damp concrete, then starts walking without waiting for her so that she has to quicken her step to catch up with him. When she is by his side, they walk together without saying anything, until the silence becomes too much.
'Where are we going?'
'We can go to your place, there is no room at my house,' he uses the word house ironically but she doesn't catch it, or is so confused by his directness that she does not know how to react.
'Isn't there a bar still open?'
She is trying to act as if nothing unusual is happening, straining not to show how awkward she feels now: saving face for him or for herself, she is not sure.
He shakes his head and smiles.
'You know, I think I'd better just go home,' she waits for his reaction but there is none. 'I feel tired,' she adds.
'If you want,' he shrugs his shoulders and stops.
She hesitates in the hush which follows the abruptness of his words, and he takes another cigarette and lights it without offering her one.
'See you around, then.'
'For sure,' he answers, smiling.
Turning, she starts to walk away, then realises that she needs to cross the road to the bus stop. She looks behind her, embarrassed at appearing confused in front of him, but he has his back to her and is already far away.

3

It is Sunday morning and he can hear the church bells ringing as he lies in bed, although they did not wake him this morning as they have so many times because he has been sleepless for the past few hours. He wonders how many people attend that church; flung so far from the city, like the refugee centre itself. He remembers a programme he once watched on State TV one bored, student afternoon, where they spoke about the formation of the Jewish ghetto in Rome. The presenter traced with his footsteps the line which the walls of the ghetto once took, explaining how a church had been built at each exit so that every time a Jew left or entered his home, he would be exposed to the words of Christ. He smiles at the idea that the local priest here, aware of the forced presence of two hundred Muslims in his parish, had a similar idea.

Now that they have nothing left to belong to anymore: no hometown, no house or job or school, many people have found their sense of belonging in the religion which they inherited through the accidents of history. He knows very well that a people's loyalty was dictated by the empire which conquered them; and they happened to be occupied by the Arabs. It is nothing more complicated than that: no divine intervention, just the political manoeuvrings of super-powers. He knows this and yet he would never admit it to a living soul; at this moment in history it is the only thing his people have left. He is also classified as a Muslim now, although he has never set foot in a mosque. His father was a staunch defender of the once-popular communist party, a firm believer that the solidarity of workers went beyond matters of religion. When he died, his mother continued the membership out of respect for his memory more than any deep conviction. She herself was brought up on a loose mixture of folk superstition coupled with a sprinkling of Muslim tradition passed on through word of mouth, rather than any formal training. Yet the very name they gave him, more a matter of taste and habit than of faith, has him branded with the mark of the crescent moon and star.

On Sunday most of the refugees stay in the centre: this is the day when the truce between them and the society that hosts them is drawn. All embassies are closed, so there is no queuing for visas; all colleges and universities are also shut, so there can be no requests for permission to study; and the market where many of them work cleaning and selling vegetables is replaced by an antiques fair this one day a week. For his people (he likes to use the possessive pronoun, it gives him an enhanced sense of belonging, as well as responsibility) Sunday is now the day of rest which they must all abide by.

Today he will follow his usual routine: take his washing to the cousin whose sense of guilt for not taking him in when he first arrived urged her to offer this weekly service. He also gets a hot meal and a living room to sit in, complete with comfy sofa and TV and a drinks cabinet in the corner. Her husband makes it his business to always be away working at his garage or at his allotment on Sundays and only comes back when lunch has long finished.

He will not go to take a shower this morning, as the bathrooms are always crowded at this time. Instead, he gets up from his bed to take his clothes from the day before, which he has carefully folded and placed on top of the chest of drawers. His two roommates are still lying in bed, although neither of them is asleep.

'Going to play house again?' asks Pale, looking at him from the adjacent bed.

Pale's real name is Peter: a Christian of Russian descent whose status as a refugee is suspect. Technically, Orthodox Christians should have nothing to fear from the pro-government militia which rule the majority of the country, but there are always personal vendettas which make life difficult for anyone with a past. Pale is safer here, in the no-man's land of asylum and he knows that none of his fellow inmates are going to report his questionable presence; that he can rely on the natural reticence which all of them share in the face of authority.

'In our position, we have to accept all that's on offer,' Azad retaliates good-humouredly, pulling out the sports bag from underneath his bed where he has stored his dirty clothes from last week. He strips the bed and takes the bedclothes too, not content with the once-a-month change which all inhabitants are entitled to. Taking hold of each sheet, he brings the corners together, folds each one into a small square, then slips them into the bag and does up the zip.

Outside the barrack his exit is blocked by washing lines loaded with damp sheets and clothes, filling the air with the strong odour of artificial freshness. The women are taking a break before they make lunch; sitting together on the stone steps drinking coffee from mugs and smoking cheap cigarettes, their patterned headscarves like flower beds amongst the grey of the concrete and brick. As he passes by, one of them winks at him, 'We'd do your washing for you, love. We could work out the price together!'

The other women laugh as she straightens herself out provocatively to reveal large breasts overflowing the top of her floral blouse and apron. Most of the women refugees came to Lithuania alone, leaving their men behind to fight. Although they all have at least two school-aged children, some of them are the same age as him. He knows from experience that if he is to survive amongst them he must ignore their advances like he ignores their rural accents and habits. This banter between them seems to be a compromise which they are all satisfied with.

'But I have a lot of washing!' he shouts back at them, making a gesture with his hand towards his crotch. He can still hear their un-self-conscious laughter as he walks up the gravel path and onto the asphalt road.

He arrives at the bus stop just in time to see the bus pulling off into the distance. On Sundays the service is reduced and he knows he must wait another hour for the next one. He considers for a minute going back to take his bike but then remembers the cumbersome bag he is carrying and decides to walk instead. There is nobody else around except for a few hitch-hikers waiting for a lift at the slip road which leads to the motorway. It is cold and they have coats and hats on, so he cannot tell what ethnicity or gender they are.

As he walks, around him flow the sounds and smells of a life to which he no longer has access. In this 'other Europe', as he likes to call it, the Europe which spent fifty years under Communist rule, things are very similar to the way it was for him back home: the close-knit family life, the home cooking of the women, the children playing in the street until darkness falls, un-tormented by crime statistics. People here still see Sunday as a day of rest and the only sounds to be heard are dogs barking or birds twittering overhead, while in the air linger the odours of boiled potatoes and cabbage, meat roasting in the oven, apples baking. Despite the fact that this is the city, he can sometimes catch the odour of back-garden bonfires wafting over from allotments.

The street where his cousin lives is lined on one side by six-storey blocks of flats and on the other by tall birch trees whose leaves have now turned brilliant yellow. When he came to the city twelve months ago, the buildings were still the generic socialist structures found all over the region: bare, grey concrete and narrow balconies on which jars of pickles were stored for the winter. Yet even in this short time they have been transforming themselves into something more than their basic function: new green balustrades have taken the places of old mesh ones; the windows have been re-fitted in double-glazed PVC; the façades have been given a layer of plaster and fresh white paint. There are even a few satellite dishes hanging off the edge of the shiny balconies.

He walks slowly to the third building in the street and presses the bell of number fourteen. He can hear the buzz of the door being released without having to speak into the interphone: in all his time here, he has not missed one Sunday visit. Getting into the lift he goes up to the last floor, where he knows the door will already be left ajar for him.

'Hey, Alma!' he calls out from the hallway; using the original version of her name and not the more Europeanised 'Ana' which she adopted when she emigrated here twenty years ago.

His cousin calls out to him from the kitchen and he walks through to where she is standing over pots and pans of cooking food. She has lighter skin and a more elongated face than most of her countrymen and there was always talk in the family of Russian blood. His mother was convinced that this is what saved her, enabling her to catch a Lithuanian husband from among the young recruits from across the USSR doing military service near her town. But typically the blessing was also viewed as a curse in disguise and explained how the un-healthiness of a mixed race marriage could never yield any children.

Today she has her curly, light brown hair pinned up from her still pretty face and is wearing a red apron over her jeans and shirt. She has grown fatter since his arrival here and he pats her plump bottom as he bends forward to kiss her cheek.

'How are you?' he asks softly, his head still close to hers.

She shrugs her shoulders as if to brush him away and nods towards a bowl of small, savoury biscuits which she has placed on the working surface.

'I made them earlier. Take some.'

He reaches out and takes a handful, then goes into the living room and sits down on the sofa. The television is already on, and he can see a young blond woman in a low-cut dress talking to enthusiastic contestants on a quiz show.

'Where's your husband?' he calls out in the direction of the small hatch which connects the living room to the kitchen. Through it, he can see a small square of Alma's body moving from fridge to stove.

'Thomas is at work,' she replies, with emphasis on the name that he avoids using.

He takes the TV control and begins to flick between the channels: more quiz shows, a live church service, a black and white cowboy film dubbed into German, adverts for slimming pills.

Alma comes in and takes the bag of washing which he has left by the coffee table. He knows from habit that she will go into the bathroom to put on the first load then re-fill the bag with the neatly ironed clothes and sheets from last week.

'Did you hear anything from back home?' she calls from the bathroom: it is a question best asked at a distance.

'Not this week - couldn't get a line.'

She comes back into the room, a frown across her broad forehead. 'Try now.'

His eyes flick away from the TV screen towards her, then back again. She sighs and pushes past his knees to reach the phone on the sideboard, then hands him the receiver. He does not like to do it like this, without time for preparation but he is, like most of his countrymen, a superstitious believer in fate. Perhaps this unprompted gesture is a sign that this time the call will go through and that all will be well.

He takes the receiver and dials the number he has known by heart since age six. There is a silence which follows the end of the pips as lines are connected and redirected, then a few seconds of static interference followed by an intermittent thudding which reminds him of the sound of grenades falling.
'No luck.'
Alma takes back the handset and replaces it.
'We'll watch the news at twelve,' she says, turning towards the kitchen.
He nods in agreement but he will try his best not to honour their arrangement. He has seen enough footage of his ravaged country to last a lifetime; feels he can no longer stomach the desperate faces of emaciated women and children. When he needs to, he prefers to listen to the short-wave radio he brought with him from home: somehow the words don't leave imprints on his mind like the images do.

***

It is past three o'clock when he leaves his cousin's apartment and her husband has still not returned. It was Thomas, not Alma, who was dead set against taking in any relatives when the war started. Predicting a long war, he claimed it was better to set the rules at the very beginning so that there would be no family arguments later.

It has become cooler now in the afternoons and he has taken to wearing a woollen cap over his thinning hair. Stopping for a moment to put it on, he bends to place the bag on the ground and feels the rush of air as a car passes by. When he looks up, he notices the plates are those of Thomas's car and he watches as it slows down and turns into the driveway he has just left. He hesitates for just a moment, then picks up the bag again and swings it over his shoulder: it is a faded sports bag with Adidas written in cracked white letters along the side and it is one of the two bags that he brought with him when he fled the war.

When he reaches the main road he is suddenly struck by the desire not to return to the barracks: on Sundays everybody remains in the centre and the over-load of humanity brings on a feeling of claustrophobia. Abruptly, he turns northwards and starts to walk towards the city. There is a place he likes to go to on weekends, where he can play a game he sometimes indulges in; going through the motions of the once familiar habits of his former life as if nothing had changed.

The café he always chooses is generic; its low half-lit ceilings and cheap plastic furniture giving it the anonymity of industrial design. The only other customers are two men seated at one of the booths which line one wall and are divided from each other by wooden partitions. He sits down at a table on the opposite side of the aisle, so he has them in his view. It is not a conscious decision, but since coming to this country he finds some feeling of safety in being able to keep people in his sight. He can tell immediately that they are also strangers just from the rhythm of their speech; a guttural, rough language which he cannot identify.

The waitress comes and he orders a beer. She is in her late fifties and her pale blue uniform is buttoned tight across her breasts and protruding belly. On her feet she is wearing canvas shoes tied up with laces around her thick ankles, which make her clumsy as she walks. When she comes back, she puts down the bottle then places a new ashtray over the full one which is already on the table, lifting them both up and pulling the dirty one away in a gesture made perfect through years of repetition. Then she leaves him alone, with only the sound of the strange language wafting over to him intermittently from the opposite table.

He takes out his packet of cigarettes and places it in front of him. It is a soft paper packet that has to be ripped open and he keeps it in his shirt pocket to stop the cigarettes inside from being squashed. He will buy a new packet tomorrow – a hard packet, with the money that Alma slipped into his laundry bag while he was watching TV. Every weekend the ritual is the same and it is something that neither of them has ever mentioned. When he is in a good mood, he sees it as one of the norms of family solidarity but there are days when he sees it as guilt money – the pay-off for keeping out of their lives. Today he is neutral; one year of living off humanitarian aid has made him accustomed to receiving.

He takes a cigarette and places it in his mouth and at the same time searches in his pocket for his lighter. Not finding it there, he gets up reluctantly and moves towards the men on the opposite table. They stop talking immediately and there is an uncomfortable pause in which he tries to choose which language to use to address them. Deciding not to talk at all, he raises his hand instead and mimes igniting a lighter. The man nearest him takes a box of matches from the table and in an unexpected gesture of good manners, lights the cigarette which is still hanging from his lips. Closer to, he can notice the moist creases in the man's forehead and the sweet smell which emanates from the thick, black hair which is gelled and combed back from his face.

The exchange is over in a matter of seconds, yet when he returns to his place he can feel that the air between them is no longer impartial; the space of possibility has been opened. Only a few seconds pass before the man who lit his cigarette has stood up and slid himself onto the bench opposite.

'Are you here alone?'

The man uses Russian, although his accent is cumbersome with the complexities of an unrelated language.

Azad does not reply, but the stranger seems unconcerned by his reticence to speak. He takes a napkin from the container on the table and pats away the beads of sweat still resting on his brow.

'You escaped from the war?'

'Yes.'

'It is not easy - a big problem for all of Europe.'

Azad notices that his companion has also got up from his seat now, but instead of joining them he turns towards the door and goes out into the street.

'I don't think Europe cares so much as long we don't come to their doors.'

The stranger grins a humourless grin and nods his head

'You are right, my friend, you are right.' Taking a packet of Marlboros from the inside pocket of his jacket; he offers them across the table. The taste is bitter and strong.

'If you need a woman to comfort you,' the man continues, 'I know many...very beautiful.'

From the same pocket he takes a manilla envelope, secured with an elastic band. Slowly, he rolls it aside to reveal a wad of Kodak photos.

The man does not push them upon him; laying them down instead on the table between them. There is a pause; a slight flinch of the hand.

'It's not my thing.'

The man looks at him without curiosity. His skin is once again shiny with humidity. 'Your choice,' he grunts, collecting up the cigarette packet and the photos in one swift movement and putting both back into his pocket.

The leather of his jacket creaks as he gets up to leave and once the door has closed behind him the waitress is again at the table.

'Do you need anything else?'

Her words are directed at him, although her eyes flit towards the door which still swings on its hinges. He has the impression that her gesture is protective, as if she perceives a feeling of solidarity with him in the face of men like them. He shakes his head and asks for the bill - he cannot feel her sense of shared morality.

Before the war, in fact ever since he was very young, he had the deep-rooted belief that his life was held together by a continuous thread. If he closed his eyes, he could see a fine silver line which traced out his destiny in this world: from childhood through to adolescence to student days, linking up all the friends and people whom he had ever known. But then his country had fallen apart and although he spends most of his energy on not thinking about what is happening there, he is sometimes overwhelmed by the incapacitating knowledge that he is alone in the world and that every thought he has or action he takes is random and horrifyingly pointless.

4

'Which one will you have?'

Benjamin gestures with a nod of his head to the pair of teenage girls sitting a few tables down from them. Even from a distance it is obvious that they are Russian; something about the sharp cheek bones, the brassy yellow of their dyed hair or perhaps the slight tarnish of otherness.

'The one in black,' Azad answers.

Benjamin looks over at the girls once more, without pausing to hide the fact that they are discussing them; 'A little chubby around the belly for me.'

'I like a bit of a belly,' he replies, 'it's the first sign of decay. I like to be reminded that all flesh, even such young flesh, is ultimately condemned.'

He realises that by saying these words he could easily have slipped across a border but Benjamin looks at him for only a brief moment before laughing dismissively. They watch the two girls as they finish their ice creams, scooping up the nearly melted strawberry goo with their spoons and slipping it between parted lips. One of them takes a serviette from the table and wipes her hands and face while the other licks her fingers.

The waiter arrives and barely hides his annoyance as he takes another order for coffee. He is back almost immediately with the plain white cup of thick, bitter liquid and the tall glass of tap water, placing them a little too roughly onto the table so that the coffee spills into the saucer. Returning to the bar, he exchanges a comment with his colleague who immediately turns towards them with a look of distaste.

'He gets paid the same whether we sit here drinking champagne or espresso.' Azad's eyes are bright with indignation as he watches the two waiters gossiping.

Benjamin looks over briefly towards the bar, following his friend's stare. 'Forget it!' he says, good-humouredly.

'People here have forgotten what they once were. Anybody would think this was Switzerland.'

He eyes the two waiters evenly and smiles to himself when they finally turn away.

'Didn't you have an appointment at the university on Friday?' Benjamin asks, leaning across the table to take the sugar. He stirs in three consecutive spoons before he gets a reply.

'They want me to do the exam to enter the third year.'

'But that's great!'

Benjamin takes his friend by the shoulder and keeps his hand there, gently rocking the unwilling body.

'I'd almost finished, back home. I'll be like an old man to the rest of my classmates.'

'How old are you?'

'Technically, twenty-seven, but I reckon it at twenty-four - one year lost to military service, one to the war and a year in this dump.'

'You should take it as a compliment that they took you at all.'

'It's not an act of charity.'

'Nevertheless,' Benjamin shrugs.

The two of them sit silent for a few moments, while behind them the girls get up from their table, laughing at an unheard joke. He looks up to watch them as they recede down the street into two indistinct figures without gender or age.

'I'd like to get laid tonight.'

'Wouldn't we all!' Benjamin lifts his cup to drink the last dregs, then puts it back on his saucer before letting a broad smile cross his lips. 'You should get a girlfriend,' he adds.

'Had one of those back home, thanks.'

'The girls here are different…and there are plenty of foreigners around…'
He looks Benjamin in the eyes now: this is the first thing he has said that has really caught his attention.
'What do you mean by that?'
'You know, they are less fucked-up about what other people think. You can have a good time with them and they aren't going to dismiss you just because of where you come from.'
He sighs at the false expectation, 'They've probably never heard of where we come from.'
Benjamin frowns, 'Seriously. It's better than facing all of this alone.'
'I'll think about it then.' His voice is soft for a change, devoid of judgement.
The two of them turn as a motorbike, its mufflers removed, speeds along the deserted Sunday streets.
'Are you going to the party tonight?' Benjamin asks, leaning across the table to take the bill.
'Probably. You?'
'Can't – I have a date. I've got to go back to the centre and shower first,' he grins expectantly, then adds 'Coming?'
'Not now. I think I'll walk around a bit then go straight to the fiesta.'
Benjamin takes some loose coins from his pocket and places them next to his cup then gets up to leave. 'Good luck tonight - don't do anything I wouldn't!'

***

There are so many people at the party that they can hardly squash into the small room which the owner of the bar has lent them for the night. The landlord is a fellow Muslim of Tatar descent whose family escaped from Russia during the civil war and settled in Turkey but never managed to prosper. In the

41

euphoria and confusion of 1989, he re-traced his grandparent's journey in reverse and ended up in the newly declared Republic of Lithuania, stopping short of his ancestral home by a few hundred kilometres.

Failing the ambitions he had for a better life, Turk has marketed himself as a sympathiser of the cause and his bar has become a meeting place for the rare and the disaffected: the last remnants of the indigenous Muslim Tartars and the newly-arrived refugees and workers from the Central Asian republics of the former USSR. His bar is popular with immigrants - a rest from the burden of foreignness which they usually have to carry with them.

Entering, Azad nods briefly to Turk and looks around the crowded room for someone he knows. The air is heavy with smoke and the rise and fall of excited chatter which competes for attention over the music. The gathering has been called in order to give a last and memorable farewell to Alan, so-named after his father's love of an Italian cartoon strip which was popular in the seventies: a useful whim which leaves him the advantage of a Christian sounding name. Alan is one of the oldest teenagers in the refugee centre and has been here since the very beginning of the war. He arrived with his younger brother, who hasn't spoken or been able to coordinate his movements since birth. The two of them have received a visa for Canada, one of the most popular destinations among the refugees. There they will be given free language courses and permission to work, as well as the promise that they can stay forever.

Alan sees him at the doorway and pulls himself away from the crowd in order to welcome him
'I didn't think you'd come,' he says, offering his hand in greeting.

The two of them shake hands and Alan leans in close for an embrace; alcohol making him demonstrative.

"I never miss a party, you know me.'

'Especially if there's free drink and nice girls, eh?' Alan teases.

Azad shrugs this off, 'I've heard there are nicer girls in Canada.'

'Maybe they're just easier to conquer…. but there are no girls nicer than ours!'

Alan's voice rises into a shout as he articulates this last observation and there is a cheer from those near enough to hear: they are all celebrating Alan tonight.

Out of the crowd a girl comes over and kisses Alan's cheek as if to prove the point and he rests his hand on her rump while he takes another swig of his beer, then he is gone, buffeted around the room between people wanting to say goodbye and those who want to remind him not to forget them once he arrives in the land of plenty. Alan is the centre of attention in this party intended to celebrate the wonderful new life of possibility he will have in the new world. It would have been considered a triumph to get a Canadian visa even before the war: there was always so little faith in the future of his nation. Yet the atmosphere is not a simple one; there is the bitterness of jealousy mixed in with the happiness and somewhere very deep, there is the dreadful trace of betrayal. Another young, healthy male leaves his people and his homeland behind.

Azad takes a beer from the bar and finds himself a corner out of the way of the main throng. Someone has started plucking at a guitar and slowly those who are seated nearby start to make requests for the traditional songs they cannot hear on the local radios or in the bars, interjecting reminiscences which randomly get taken up or ignored by the rest of the group. These melodies are the standard feature of any party organized by his countrymen; full of the sad longing and pathos of people thrust into an unwanted place.

Next to him are two girls whom he knows by sight, as they run a makeshift hairdressing service at the refugee centre. He has seen them on fine days, laying newspaper on the ground and setting up chairs for customers to sit on while they clip and trim in efficient, humourless movements. Typically, they both have over-dyed, over-worked hair which stays tight and static despite the humidity of the room. Now that the singing has started, they have become tearful with a nostalgia accentuated by alcohol.

Leaning towards the one nearest to him, he clinks his bottle against hers,
'What's your name?'
'Zahra'
He nods in approval and notices that she has almond-shaped eyes, reminiscent of Turkish women. Her face is smooth and untroubled and he estimates that she cannot be much older than twenty.
'You're the student, aren't you?'
She observes him as he laughs in response: approving his rounded cheekbones and sharp fine nose, and noticing the unusual green eyes which make him so attractive. Even at the centre she had noticed his precariously thin figure making its way across the forecourt; his look of concentration as he manoeuvred his bicycle between the barracks and chained it dutifully against the mesh fence.
'Is that what they call me?'
She blushes slightly, 'it's a compliment, I think.'
He smiles and watches her as she sways slightly from intoxication. Shyly, her eyes avoid his but her body leans in towards him lethargically. Imperceptibly, he shuffles closer, letting his arm brush lightly against hers.

The two of them remain like this for some time, listening to the music, sometimes singing along; all the while their skin growing accustomed to the feel of the other. He has learnt to estimate the moment of attack quite accurately and it is only when the movement of the party's lifespan has reached its peak and is slowly winding downwards, that he makes his move.

'Can I accompany you home?'

She looks at him with a mock shyness and nods. When they get up to leave, he sees her wink to her friend.

Outside, the reverie of the party is replaced by the reality of late night drunks making their way home along the shabby streets which surround the railway station. The pavement is littered with small groups of men sharing bottles of cheap vodka or brandy and traders from across the border selling un-labelled blister packs of pills from plastic bags stuffed with pharmaceutical cartons. Sensing a sudden lack of nerve from Zahra at the abrupt shift in reality, he takes her by the hand and hails a taxi; an extravagance which he has only allowed himself on one previous occasion. His motivation is two-fold: this way he will score more points in her estimation and he will also avoid the risk of meeting any fellow refugees on the bus ride home. Gossip among his people, who have nothing to do but observe each other every hour of every day, can be vicious.

When they arrive at the centre, he leads her to the door of Blacky's room, at the far end of his corridor. He has a special arrangement with Blacky, whose mother works as a live-in housekeeper outside of town, leaving him the sole occupancy. Knocking gently on the door, he takes her hand and then withdraws to down the corridor without saying a word. Feeling self-conscious, she lets herself be led by him and waits in silence. After a few minutes Blacky comes out in T-shirt and shorts, his hair swept up and his eyes full of sleep. He mutters something towards the figures at the end of the hallway and retreats back into the room but they do not move. After a few more minutes he comes out again, this time carrying bed sheets and blankets in his arms, and walks away from them down the corridor where they see him disappear into another room.

He catches Zahra's arm loosely now and pulls her after him. It is dark inside and he doesn't bother to turn on the light. Leaning over towards her, he cups his hand behind her head and pulls her forward to kiss. Her lips taste sweet from the beer and her body leans in closer towards him without resistance. It is an easy kiss, without any of the self-conscience of pride at stake: he is out of her league and she knows it.

Beneath the embrace his hands as they move slowly beneath the material of her shirt. She is already out way further than her family or her upbringing allows; but the ragged loneliness of exile has made her defiant. And when she dares to feel his skin, she is shocked at the strange thinness it. Despite knowing that he is older than her, she is nevertheless unprepared for the texture of his flesh which seems already old; slightly loose from the bones as if the force of gravity has begun to win its lifelong battle prematurely.

Verging dangerously close to the unmarked borders of her own chastity, she pulls back from him and straightens her clothes.
'I have to get back to my room.'
He looks at her young flushed face and smiles, despite himself.
'Can't you stay just five more minutes? Look,' he takes the pack of cigarettes and offers her one, then lights up for the both of them. 'I promise I won't try anything – just lie down with me for a while and we can speak.'

Leaning back on the bed together he strokes her arm absent-mindedly and talks about anything that seems to come into his head: his childhood, his year of military service, his plans to finish his studies. There is no expectation of a response from her, she is just the audience to this unburdening of his personality, and she experiences a sense of relief at the lack of obligation. He doesn't ask for her surname, or if she is alone or with her family, for things don't need a lot of explanation here: everybody knows why you have come and what you have left behind. They all share the common decision not to stay and fight - even the women are not exempt, for there are plenty of females who are prepared to give up their lives in defence of their home or their faith.

5

His room is dark and quiet when he wakes; his two roommates still sleeping and the radiators softly clicking and gurgling as the heating kicks into action. He gets up cautiously and takes his shower bag and towel from the cabinet, then creeps out into the corridor. Across the hallway a door opens and Benjamin comes out on his way to the bathrooms, wearing just his T-shirt and boxer shorts. An old woman, passing back from the female cubicles, looks at him disapprovingly and mutters something about keeping standards.

'What the hell are you doing up so early?' Benjamin asks, peering outside at the darkness which hasn't yet yielded to day.

'What are you doing?' he retaliates, 'I thought you had a date.'

Benjamin sighs and shrugs his shoulders, 'I can't stay every night. Her bloody flatmate isn't too keen on that arrangement.'

'You could always bring her back here…'

Benjamin looks at him, incredulous, 'So she can snuggle up with my sister and my mother, like?'

Azad laughs and moves towards the shower: he has to finish before the rush of workers getting ready for the first shift.

By the time he has washed and shaved it is already light and the place is bustling with movement. The air is scented with the smell of boiling coffee and alive with the constant sound of running water as each inhabitant takes his turn in the communal showers. He must go to the faculty today to collect the letter left for him by the dean and take it to the Director of the Engineering Department. For this he must be clean and well dressed; clean-mouthed too, for he cannot afford to make any enemies at this stage.

Once he has put on the laundered, ironed clothes he took from Alma's, he feels more ready to face the world: after all, he is only in his twenties and there is everything still to achieve. The air outside is crisp with the promise of a long, mild autumn and the sky is bright blue. In front of the canteen barrack he can see the industrial food vats being carried out and loaded into the back of a waiting van which carries the logo of the local catering company that won the government tender to provide daily meals to the refugee population.

Behind the van, he can see the silent line of young males waiting patiently for the dining room to be cleared. Each one wears a crocheted, white skull cap on his head and clasps a small worn book in his hands. These are the members of the religious school started by the resident imam, already long retired but inspired back into service by the growing need of the increasingly disillusioned population. Since the beginning of the year he has held classes every morning for three hours, after which there is a special lunch cooked on site and funded by an Islamic aid organisation from Saudi Arabia. Ismail, one of the founding members, stands at the front of the queue, his head slightly askance as if to avoid the gaze of the few women who wander out of the building reluctantly, their breakfast over and four hours to kill until the next meal.

He has been asked to join the school twice; the first time by Ismail on the day that they were allotted a room together. The second time was a month later, when the elderly imam called all the male residents together in order to express the need for organised religious education in order to counteract the harmful influences of the morally corrosive host society. It is a practice tolerated by the camp authorities on the condition that its activities remain within the centre and do not infringe on its daily running. The imam and his contacts understand that as prospective entrants into the European Union the Lithuanian government must be seen to respect the rights of all its population, no matter how temporary. On one occasion, there had been a delegation sent from the Lithuanian office of United Nations High Commissioner for Refugees: two large white jeeps proudly bearing the proud blue logo and diplomatic number plates rolled up to the office building and spat out a line of grim-faced officials who marched into the administrative offices and marched out two hours later. The imam had worn his best robes and the men from the self-appointed resident's council had taken out their brown suits and typed out a list of their demands on an antiquated portable typewriter donated by the Red Cross.

He has noticed, despite his desire to ignore it, that the queue of earnest young men has grown over the last few months. Simultaneously, the heads of the population have been gradually coloured with the white of the male skull-cap or the dark blue and black of headscarves. In his mind he tries to identify the turning point; the exact time which announced a shift in consciousness. He has watched American TV shows proclaiming the 'end of innocence' with the sensational images of melting metal and fire, but for him it seems a far more gradual process: a growing tension, a nursed grudge, the collective memory of a people thwarted and impoverished.

Taking his bicycle from where he always locks it to the chain fence, he pedals slowly along the gravel track towards the main road. The thin trees and bushes of the surrounding waste ground soon yield to the hard lines and right-angles of the garages and warehouses of the city suburbs. In only a matter of minutes, the camp and its politics are consigned to the miserable corner of obscurity which they have been allotted. Once he is on the main road to the city centre he loosens the gears and rides at full speed. Keeping his mind blank, he can almost believe that he is a legitimate part of the morning traffic, an integral element in the working parts of the city.

***

The secretary is not prepared for his arrival and doesn't notice his presence as she fixes her lipstick in a small hand mirror that she holds just above the desk. Looking up at the sound of his coughing, she is momentarily left bare without the armour of her usual role.
'There should be a letter waiting for me from the Dean.'
He has prepared the sentence well and there is only the slightest hint of an accent hovering inside it. By the time he has delivered it, her face has regained its look of superiority and she takes an envelope from her desk and slides it only half way across the table, so that he has to lean forward to take it.
'Your personal data has already been in-putted into our system. If you pass the necessary entrance tests, your student account will be automatically activated.'
Satisfied that she has shown him she knows who he is, she moves her gaze back towards the papers on her desk. He pauses for a moment and is about to ask her for the directions for the Mechanical Engineering department but changes his mind. Remembering the notice board in the main hall, he retraces his steps to the ground floor.

The foyer is full of students huddled together in little groups, talking and laughing and exchanging papers between classes. In one corner is a stall selling handmade crafts for an animal charity; greetings cards and T-shirts from which the forlorn faces of beagles and rabbits plead for rescue. A young female student, all smooth skin and smiles, rattles a collection box towards him and asks for a contribution. His attraction to her is only slightly stronger than his anger at the gross hypocrisy of this society.

Usually he would relish a tirade as to why Western people spend millions on their pets when people in his own country have hardly enough food to survive. But there is a naïve eagerness about her expression which holds him back, and with a concerted effort he simply waves his hand dismissively and moves away: today, after all, is a new start for him.

Turning, he makes his way towards the notice board and checks the code number of his course. The head of his department is located on the third floor of the right wing of the faculty and he takes the stairs up, preferring them always to the lift: fear of being trapped in enclosed spaces is one of the phobias he developed during the bombing and he automatically steers clear of such places with the instinct of a cat avoiding water.

When he arrives outside the door, he can see through the glass that the director is not alone; there are a dozen students seated around his large desk, their notebooks rested on their laps or balanced on the raised thigh of a crossed leg. His does not try to catch the professor's eye, turning immediately and seating himself on the bench which has been placed against the opposite wall. The corridor is silent except for the low buzzing of a vending machine at the other end. He wishes that he had brought a book, as he imagines the sight of him sitting unoccupied will not work in his favour. He must be calculating in his every move now; for he is acutely aware that this is one of the few chances he has left to alter the course of his life.

He only has to wait ten minutes until the door opens and the students file out into the corridor. There are several females – all peach skin and loose hair – who look at him briefly as they pass and he cannot help but notice the smell of them: it is not the musty odour of the camp but something fresh and slightly sweet. When they have all disappeared down the stairwell, he takes the letter out of his bag and holds it out in front of him like a passport at a border. When he knocks at the door there is a pause before a voice from inside tells him to enter. The professor does not look up from the desk where he is writing.

'Excuse me,' Azad prompts.

It is perhaps the accent which causes the professor to put down his pen and look up with a curiosity. His eyes reveal a certain warmness which is not lost on Azad's often over-sensitive judgement.

'Can I help you?'

'I have a letter for you from the Dean.'

He ventures forward and hands over the envelope, then adds 'it's about the continuation of my studies.'

The professor starts to tear at the brown paper and pulls out the letter from inside. It takes him what seems like a long time to read it through till the end, and when he has finished he folds it carefully back into its envelope.

'You want to enter the third year,' he states, rather than asks.

'That is what the Dean suggested.'

The professor smiles ever so slightly and nods as if in agreement. 'You will have already studied most of what we'll be covering but that will give you time to catch up with the language. Get a copy of the timetable and the reading list from the library on the floor below. I will arrange for you to take the second year exam next Tuesday...' he pauses for a moment to consult the large, open diary on his desk, then scribbles something quickly in pencil 'at nine o'clock. It takes about two hours.'

He hands back the envelope to Azad and gives the impression that the matter is closed, then adds 'think of it as revision – you've probably not done any studying for a while.'

Exiting the classroom and closing the door behind him, Azad allows a smile to pass across his lips. The interview lasted only a matter of minutes, yet he feels lighter; almost contented. He tucks the letter carefully back into his bag with the conscious decision to keep safe all the documentation he is given – he will not let history cheat him again. Returning to the stairwell he goes down to the floor below. The library seems to take up the entire length of the building, and when he enters he notices the unfamiliar hush of learning hovering in the air. The only noise seems to be the shuffling of papers as the librarian goes about his work, and for a few moments he stands motionless, taking in a peacefulness which he had almost forgotten existed.

'Can I have the timetable and the reading list for second year of Mechanical Engineering?'

The librarian looks up to face him and there is the slightest twitch of recognition in his eyes: there is something about his Asiatic features and his familiar gestures which suggest a compatriot. Turning, he surveys the piles of papers which are stacked along the wall, takes a sheet from the top of two of them, then pauses.

'Second year, did you say?'

'That's right.'

Cautiously, they speak to each other in Lithuanian. There are many reasons not to venture out into the potential misunderstandings of trying to talk in their native tongue and perhaps their instinct is wrong after all: everywhere south of here, skins are darker. Azad takes the proffered forms and looks through the list of authors. Most of them are familiar to him from his previous studies but there are some new titles which he will have to read in order to prepare for the exam. He is painfully conscious of how much each one costs: money which he guards as his only security.

'Can I take out these books?' he asks, leaning over the counter and underlining with his finger the titles he needs.

'Do you have a pass? I could issue you with a library card.'

'I won't get one till next week and then only if I pass the exam.'

54

The librarian sucks his lips, then turns quickly to look over his shoulder.

'I don't have the money for.....'Azad starts to explain, but the librarian raises his hand as if to stop his confession,

'I can give you a temporary weekly pass – it's what we issue to visiting lecturers but...' He stops mid sentence, then shrugs his shoulders as if to show that it is not him who is guilty but some higher power. Taking a small, rectangular piece of card from a drawer he begins to write the date in blue ink then passes the pen and paper quickly across the counter. 'Just fill this in,' he explains.

Azad takes the pen between his fingers and begins to write. He has to remember to use the Latin alphabet and not the Cyrillic one which they were made to use in school. Inside, his mind is smiling, for here is yet another piece of paper that will define his life. When he hands it back, the librarian feeds it carefully through a small machine which encases it in plastic, then takes it gingerly between thumb and forefinger and wafts it until it is cool. 'Here,' he says finally, passing it over, 'the books you need are all filed from 622 onwards - far left-hand corner.'

Taking it from the outstretched hand, he nods in appreciation. It is better that the two of them remain like this; safe in the neutrality of a strange tongue, unaware of their respective backgrounds and history. Like this, they can be the comrades they once were and not members of ideological groups which are now bent on each other's destruction.

6

'Your time is up.'
He has hardly raised his eyes from the desk since the start of the exam and the warning to stop comes as a surprise. With a feeling of dissatisfaction, he rests the pen on the desk and gathers together the spare sheets of paper that need to be carefully inserted into the exam booklet. The professor smiles briefly and nods in approval.
'That's it, I'm afraid.'
'Thank you,' he answers, scraping the chair as he stands and unhooking his bag from the back of the seat.
'How did you find it?'
There is a note of sympathy in the professor's voice: two hours of quiet observation have perhaps made him curious.
'Like you said, a lot of it I remembered from before but I also revised.'
The professor squints slightly, as if trying to get him into better focus.
'Come to me on Thursday morning before classes…let's say seven thirty…and I'll give you your results,' he pauses thoughtfully, 'hopefully we'll be seeing each other soon.'

Once the classroom door is closed, he can relax his muscles again. He was lying to the professor: he has spent every hour of the last few days desperately studying and trying to recall facts and figures long buried under the refuse of his displaced life. From eight in the morning till six at night he found a corner desk in one of the city libraries amongst the unread works of Lithuanian authors and scholars and during the evenings he would prop himself up uncomfortably in bed, a handkerchief covering the small bedside lamp in an attempt to minimise the disturbance to his roommates. The habit of studying is not an easy one to get back and he has had to fight with himself for the will to continue. The habit of writing is also rusty and his hand hurts from the effort of two hours movement.

He will not worry about the results of his exam; for there is a system of locks and valves which keeps him afloat and he has already set them in motion. The door to the part of his brain where he will store this great hope has already been sealed off and the only thing he will keep in mind is the requirement to be there first thing on Thursday morning, after which that room will be locked or opened for good. He must wait another forty-eight hours to hear the verdict on his life. If he has been successful, he will be able to collect his acceptance papers and be given a student pass and a library card: papers which will finally give him an identity in this country. More than this, he will have a place to come to every morning; something he needs more than a diploma or letters after his name.

Descending into the foyer he notices that the building is far more crowded today than on his first visit. It is already October and the students have all returned from their long summer holidays: huddling around the notice boards; queuing outside the administration offices; gathering in small groups to smoke on the wide steps which lead down to the road. Soon he could be one of them and yet they still seem so distant; he lacks the spark of imagination which would project his own image into their world.

Now that it is over he has no-one with whom to share his relief. He thinks of Zahra, no doubt busy in one of the barracks clipping away at the strange heads of unknown men and women. He could not go to her anyway, could not openly expose himself to the stare of his compatriots. They have only managed to meet a few short times since that first night; stealing half an hour of closeness in Blacky's unoccupied room during mealtimes or the rare occasions when her parents attend prayers without her. He must find ways to keep their relationship a secret in a place of no secrets; where every phone call and visit and stray word is noticed and reported.

Out in the street again, the sun has belatedly burst through the clouds to give a few hours of golden light before the ever-encroaching evening draws in. Ignoring his parked bicycle, he goes into the shop to buy cigarettes and a can of beer. Outside, he pulls off the ring-pull and lets the gaseous liquid slip down his throat: it is lukewarm and tinged with the metallic taste of the can. When it is finished, he twists the thin metal in his hand and tosses it into the waste bin. He has nowhere to go but back to the barracks, yet he does not want to break the spell just yet. Taking a cigarette from the new hard cover pack, he lights it up and relished the feeling of the smoke filling his lungs.

On the other side of the street a group of women and children rummage through the black, plastic bins which have been left out for collection. There are four of them, all with the dilapidated look of un-healthiness about them. The two boys wear jeans and T-shirts despite the chill, while the women are clothed in nylon and denim – the cheap, tacky Turkish clothing which they sell in every market and street stall. While the women hold open the lids of the containers, the little ones greedily disembowel the contents onto the pavement at their feet. He knows that they are looking for glass bottles which you can return to the store to retrieve the small deposit that is automatically added at the checkout. Some kids at the centre also earn their pocket money this way - collecting coins for sweets or the collection cards they are crazy about. Every now and then one of the adults catches them and there is hell to pay: his people are dark and too often mistaken for gypsies, a comparison that they detest.

When the women have managed to fill their plastic bags, they hastily move away, leaving the street pocked with bits of paper and scrap. He watches an old lady from the upper floor of the building open her window and start to shout down at the top of their retreating heads. She uses the names for them which must be common to every language but they do not react; protected as they are in the folds of a practised, ancient indifference.

He turns to unlock his bicycle from the lamp-post and sits astride it. In one quick movement he checks the traffic and darts across the road: there is nothing now except the rush of air on his face and the rhythm of his legs as he turns the pedals. Rejecting the idea of begging for the last dregs of lunch back at the centre, he heads back towards town and Turk's bar: now that he has the taste for alcohol, he will celebrate this day alone.

It is dark and dank inside Turk's bar, despite the brightness of the sun outside. The floor is still sticky and the music is loud, as if the last group of revellers had only just abandoned it to the daylight. Reluctantly, Turk turns the stereo off and takes his order. Apart from him, there is only one other customer: a heavy-set man in track suit and anorak, sipping coffee at a table in the far corner.

Azad sits himself at the bar, shy of the feigned formality of the table and chairs. The beer is straight from the fridge and for a few seconds its coldness sets his teeth on edge before the warm feeling of looseness takes over. Relaxing, his eyes wander absently towards the smeared plate glass windows and the deserted street beyond, so that he doesn't even notice the figure approaching him from behind.
'Bullshit!'
He turns towards the man who now stands beside him but doesn't answer. Up close, he can see that he has the heavy

59

features of the south; a Russian or a Georgian, although the word he used is Lithuanian.

The man looks down at him and nods knowingly, then sits down clumsily on the adjacent stool.

'You look like someone who understands.'

'Understands what?'

'All this: the simple fact that all this,' the man lets his arms stretch out towards the dirty glass, 'is bullshit.'

Azad laughs and takes another long sip of his beer, 'You've been going all night?'

The man's big hands rub together as he tries to recall the events which have led him here; as if he is preparing an apology for his own existence. Up this close, the reek of alcohol on his breath is almost overwhelming.

'Ach, the Lithuanians are not real drinkers. They always quit too early.'

'I didn't think too many Lithuanians came here...'

'True, and those that do are not the ones you would want as your friends,' he pauses and then leans forward across the stained wood, 'nor as your enemies either!'

The large face contorts into a laugh which draws in his head and shoulders but is over as soon as it has begun. 'But we can never choose our enemies; otherwise we would not have chosen the Russians.'

'Where are you from?'

'Can you not tell?' the rumpled features seem to collect themselves and take on a kind of dignity, 'Lithuanians assure me that you can always tell.'

'I'm not Lithuanian.'

The man screws up his eyes in an exaggerated gesture of concentration,

'I suppose you wouldn't be here if you were!'The man laughs briefly and then seems to loose his point of gravity. His watery eyes flick into the distance and for a moment it seems as if he has forgotten where he is, then he sways slightly and comes back into focus.

'I'm Chechen. Came here in what they call the first Chechen war – in 1996.'

'You've been here since then?'

There is something desperate in the tone of Azad's voice, a dreadful realisation of the possible longevity of exile.

'I wanted to go back a few years ago but then it all started up again. Now there's nowhere to go back to.'

'You're lucky to be here.'

The man turns on him and studies his face; then breaks out into a smile of recognition. 'That's what they say, eh? And who are we to disagree: lucky to be alive; lucky to have food in our bellies!'

Suddenly jovial, he turns towards Turk, who has taken a chair at a table in the corner and laid out the morning papers in front of him.

'Get the man some vodka!' he gestures towards Azad, 'and one for me, while you're at it.'

Reluctantly, Turk gets up from his seat and takes two small, clear glasses from under the counter, which he fills with the transparent liquid. The two of them knock them back in one gulp then remain silent while the burning feeling inside them dies down.

'I see that they named a square in Vilnius after Dudayev,' Azad ventures.

'They even let his wife live here. The Lithuanians know what it's like to fight the Russians - they kept up their resistance till the 50's…. ah, you have to hand it to the Russians - they've kept us by the balls for more than 150 years.'

'You respect them after all?'

'I respect their damned Slavic belief in themselves, their willingness to sacrifice for greater Russia in whatever form.'

'Respect: that's a tall order.'

'We have more reason to hate them than you, my friend. The Central Asians didn't do so badly, but us Chechens...ha! We are too tough for our own good. We can go on fighting even when there is nothing left to fight for.'

Azad starts at the recognition, uncomfortable at being labelled, but the man brushes it aside with his laugh and slaps his hand down onto the bar.

'You would do well to learn from us,' a big paw lands on his shoulder and rests there, while the man takes the vodka bottle from behind the bar and with his other hand and pours out two more glasses. Turk looks up from his papers briefly but remains silent.

'Do you know what they did to us? How Stalin punished us for our rebellion during the Second World War?'

Azad shakes his head and stares at the large rough hands; the stern face sagging with tiredness and alcohol.

'They transported us – the whole lot of us: women and children – took us from our homes and sent us to Siberia. Half of them died on route from cold and hunger.'

In his inebriation there is no difference between the past and the present; the 'them' of sixty years ago and the 'us' of now - it has all become blurred into one undeniable litany of oppression.

'Had you heard about that before? They weren't allowed back till Khrushchev came to power – twelve years later. That's not something that was ever taught during communism, eh?'

'No, that's the first time I've heard it.'

The Chechen nods knowingly, his head ducking a little too low at every incline so that it has to be jerked up again in an awkward movement. 'Now you see what you are up against.'

'I take it you don't see the point in staying and fighting?'

'Being a soldier.... that's for some people. But there are other ways to serve your country - soldiers need guns and ammunition. There have to be ways of getting the means to fight to the ones who have to fight, if you know what I mean...'

Suddenly, the figure of Turk is behind them, taking the still-full glasses of vodka from the bar and pouring the contents into the sink.

'You've had enough.'

The man looks at him and then at Turk, his bushy eyebrows knitted together in petulance.

'You don't need to worry. I can choose my drinking partners even when I'm drunk. We are all Muslims here...'

'Nevertheless.'

The Chechen hesitates, his large form bowing slightly as if submitting to some passing breeze.

'I'm here almost everyday,' he leans in close enough to whisper, 'if you should ever need anything...a brother in need, as we say...'

'That's enough,' Turk moves around the bar to where the man is standing and ushers the unwilling body out into the daylight.

***

The afternoon light is already fading when he returns to the refugee centre and there is a dull lethargy in the bodies which dawdle slowly between the buildings and congregate around the front steps of the barracks. He can hear the muttering of the women drifting through the cooling air; bemoaning the changing of the seasons and the approach of winter, reminiscing over the familiar talisman of town names and native food - the reverberations of their endless conversations like a mantra accompanying every waking hour. Gently, he secures his bike and retraces his steps back to the room, which he finds blissfully empty. Taking off his shoes and coat, he lies down on the bed to rest before the evening meal is served.

He must have been asleep for no more than ten minutes when the door is suddenly thrust open and a child of about twelve sticks his face between the parted wood.

'There's a call for you.'

He groans at being woken, then swings his legs onto the floor and reaches over to the cabinet for his cigarettes.

'It's international,' the boy emphasises, leaving the door ajar as he runs back into the courtyard. Azad looks briefly at the swinging door, then gets up slowly from the bed. He is reluctant to miss the few precious moments of solitude while his roommates are still absent and irked by the interruption of an unexpected call.

Slipping his feet into his trainers without undoing them, he steps out on the linoleum of the corridor. It is wet, and at the far end of the hallway he can see two women resting on their heals and wiping the floor with damps cloths. There is a daily rota for cleaning whereby two women are made responsible for every communal floor and surface. It is an unwinable battle, for the grime of two hundred people packed into six hundred square metres cannot be removed with old rags and bleach. It is only the air that changes, from the dankness of old shoes and fried food to a mask of chemical freshness.

The phone which is designated for communal use is located in the office block; the only new building in the compound. Its breeze block and plaster structure took ten days to construct, during the first two weeks of their arrival, and in it were placed the offices of the director and the social worker, as well as a small room containing a telephone which receives in-coming calls only. It is not a private place, for there is always someone on duty to take the calls, along with those who have nothing better to do than monitor who talks to whom and how often.

When he enters, there are five people clustered around the small table and the windows are thrown open onto the curious faces of those who spend their days in the courtyard knitting and playing cards. He is a rare visitor here, for phone calls from his country are expensive and he prefers his mother to keep the little she has for essentials. The only reason she would call would be in an emergency.

He takes the receiver from the outstretched hand of the man on duty and tries to turn away from the eyes that are fixed on him.
'Hello?'
'Is that you?' A voice cuts through his consciousness to the raw flesh of memory: it is not a voice he expected to hear again in his life.
'How did you find me?'
It is an odd question, where perhaps more tender words are in order. She was, after all, the only woman whom he ever told he loved.
'We still have friends in common,' her voice has aged and he has the feeling that she is talking to him from a great distance.
'Where are you now?'
'Where I should be.' She pauses, perhaps trying hard not to retrace old patterns, 'what about you?'
'As you can see.'
'Have you changed your mind yet?'
He doesn't answer her question and in the stillness he can hear the crackling of electricity down the line. His gaze is fixed upon the uneven whitewash of the wall; it is as if he can suddenly see every sweep of the brush and every fleck of dust imprinted there.
'Do you still feel disengaged? That this is not your war?'
'What do you want?'
'There are people who would like very much to get in contact with you. If you had the right feelings towards them…'

'You know very well that I have never been interested in that cause,' his voice is low but insistent and he is aware of a shuffle of movement from the bodies behind him.

'Have you seen what the government are doing to our people? How the world sits back and does nothing? Do you think they would be so afraid to help if it weren't Muslims being slaughtered…?'

He can recognise the old anger in her voice, the sense of injustice un-revenged.

'You know as well as I do that it's not so simple.'

A short, sharp laugh makes its way to him down the line and he flinches involuntarily.

'I know what I know, but I just wanted to check.'

'Check what?'

She hesitates and although the words she speaks are gentle, he cannot recognise her in them. 'If you were alive.'

There is no time for goodbyes: the line is cut with the suddenness of death. He puts down the receiver and turns to the door; uncharacteristically self-conscious as he avoids the expectant stares.

Outside, the light seems uncommonly bright and for a brief moment he feels as if he is going to faint. He falters only slightly, perhaps not even enough for people to notice but enough for him to feel the panic of vulnerability.

It seems to him that he cannot get enough air into his lungs and he breathes in short, shallow gulps. It is only when he has negotiated the crowded corridor, nodded to the faces he knows, stepped over the discarded bucket of cooling water and entered his room, that he feels he can breath normally again. Without the presence of mind to check if he is alone or not, he sinks to his knees against the closed wood of the door, his hands holding the sides of his head.

He stays like this for some minutes, listening to the urgency of his breathing subside into a steady rhythm. When he lifts his eyes from the patch of floorboard where they have been focused, he is already recovered enough to feel grateful that the room is unoccupied. Pulling himself to his feet, he surveys the space around him: there are only three square metres which he could really call his own – the bed and the bedcovers, the small chest of drawers, the suitcase and sport's bag under the bed and half a wardrobe of clothes. He sees it all now as she would see it; as a pitiful compensation for the pride he relinquished when he registered himself as a refugee.

There is an argument going inside his head; one which has been constant for almost two years. Sometimes it is audible and sometimes it is not, but it is continuous and insistent. Now it has reached an almost deafening level of intensity: there are voices which accuse and intimidate, others which try to placate, then there are the aggressive tones of the bully and the denials of the lair. He is a deserter, a coward, a traitor; he is a victim, a conscientious objector, a person beyond the idiocy of politics. But way down at the baseline, there is the unflinching desire for survival which will not be dislodged: it is the anchor to which he is tethered and so long as it remains tight the arguments will never pull him away from the shore.

7

It is early morning and the town is still sunken into a fine mist which seems to cling to his legs as he kicks through it. He tells himself that this is northern weather, as heavy and predictable as the grey stone buildings that squat along the roadside with their peeling facades. There is no long autumn here like there is at home but simply a sudden shift from the rainy summer's end to the fogs and frost of a long winter. This is his second winter here, yet ironically he told himself he was only coming for a few months while the situation at home calmed down: the fighting had become so bad by then that even a trip to the shop could be fatal.

In his home town, this is the time of year when the housewives would be collecting tomatoes and peppers and boiling them into a sauce which they will can and store for when there is no fresh produce to be found. He can exactly recall the smell of his mother's home; the bitter-sweet combination which boiled slowly on the flame for hours, seeping into the fabric of the chairs and blankets. His memory grows apricots, apples, quince, and almonds; the colours and odours of a ripeness which peaks before the inevitable crashing down of winter.

At the bus stop, there is the usual early-morning mix of workers going to, or returning from, their jobs. He has learnt to recognise the night workers easily; their unnatural paleness from hours spent under the glow of neon lights, their eyes staring as if they see nothing, as if they have already closed down and are sleeping while still managing to stand up. These are the poorest of the Lithuanians and the minorities who live outside of the mainstream of society: the Poles, the Russians with their bad

Lithuanian, the Ukrainians and the Byelorussians. Some of them clutch thin plastic bags containing the day's purchases; bread and milk and tinned foods, along with bottles of cheap cherry vodka and plum brandy.

The rest of the people are limited to sour-faced local women in their fifties; a generation he has come to hate. He imagines that all over the territory of the former socialist empire you can find the same breed, all wearing nylon suits and square heeled shoes, fake leopard skin blouses and pastel jackets with shoulder pads. They are a generic type: school teachers and civil servants and middle managers born of the past regime and too old to take their fashion from the new boutiques and chain stores that have blossomed since the arrival of 'freedom'. With their persistent old-school belief that all workers are equal, they treat everyone with the same impatient disgust from exactly seven a.m. till three in the afternoon, with no consideration of career advancement. Unwilling to relinquish their power, they continue to occupy the seats of almost every public function while an impatient new generation eagerly awaits their retirement. It is not EU entry which will really change Lithuania, he likes to tell people, but the death of these bastions of the old order.

In the distance he can hear the church bells chime six o'clock and several of the women bend their heads towards their wrists and reset their watches. Out of the corner of his eye he notices a figure which he recognises even through the folds of her raincoat. Lucy: something inside him shifts its weight and he looks around him nervously, as if his reaction had been visible. He has not seen her since that night at the club.

She is even paler this morning, concentrating on some private dialogue which draws her expression inwards, so that she doesn't notice as he approaches her from behind. He circles his hands

around her to cover her eyes, in a movement so gentle that it neutralises any trace of surprise. His touch is so light that the tenderness of it makes her shiver (does his skin actually touch hers or is it just the sensation of proximity?). She raises her hand to take his and turns to face him, their fingers briefly clasped.
'You startled me... I know so few people here,' she stammers.
'You looked lonely.'
'I was just thinking about how sad everything seems now that the seasons have changed.'

He is stopped from replying by her backwards glance and sees the figure of Benjamin emerging from the bar behind them. Instinctively he moves away from her, but Benjamin is carrying a coffee in each hand and his eyes are cast downwards towards the hot plastic cups. It is only when he is close that he looks up and smiles in recognition and there is nothing about his demeanour which shows that he has seen anything of what passed between them.
'What are you doing out this early?'
Benjamin hands Lucy her cup although his gaze remains fixed on his friend.
'I'm now officially a student and today I still have to read the lecture notes before my eight o'clock class.'
"You're joking!' Benjamin's hand rises into the air and falls down onto his shoulder in a gesture of unconcealed delight. He turns to Lucy and translates;
'This bastard passed his exams to enter university and he didn't even tell me...but as you can see, I am a real friend who forgives him and is just happy for his success.'
Lucy's eyes, which have avoided contact since Benjamin's arrival, now turn to his,
'Congratulations.'
He smiles despite himself, and jerks his head towards Benjamin,

'He is never in the centre to tell - he has better places to be, I think.'

She blushes, as he intended her to but Benjamin just laughs, emptying his cup and discarding it in the bin, then tucking his shirt loosely into his jeans. It is only a brief gesture, yet it is enough: he knows that the two of them must be returning from her flat after spending the night together.

'This is my bus,' he states, a little too quickly.

'You don't have to run away,' Benjamin speaks in their own tongue again, leaving Lucy outside their conversation.

'Don't won't to spoil the atmosphere...'

As the vehicle moves away, he can see the two of them move close to kiss. He turns his head away from the window and leans back onto the hard wooden seat; confused by his own desire for a foreign woman whose background and upbringing are so different to his. But perhaps it is that foreignness that appeals to him, the fact that she is removed from the others by her lack of knowledge; knowledge of all that his people have lived through in recent years – the break-up of the USSR, the inflation and the poverty, the rising sense of desperation to find a nationality or a cause to belong to, the war..... And with a sudden jolt of realisation, he understands that it is this absence of suffering in her that he finds so compelling. He almost laughs at the thought: she is like Eve before the apple - not innocent in the sexual sense but innocent of pain. His desire is almost a perverted sense of nostalgia, as if in the folds of her sex he could find a way back to that time when the world seemed to make sense, to a time when there still seemed something to hope for.

***

He was avoiding the truth when he told Benjamin that he still had to study for his lecture. The reason for his leaving the centre so early is that today is the day that he always calls his mother from the post office, and he likes to be the first in the queue for when it opens at seven. From experience he has learned that the chances of getting a line are greater at the beginning of the day, when the ageing Russian exchanges are not overloaded with business calls.

In his mother's house there is a blue, plastic dial phone resting on the dining room table in pride of place. It is one of thousands of identical phones which can be seen in almost every middle-class home across his country; the only model once available in the official state-run department stores. He knows its charmless ring so well that he can exactly imagine it clanging throughout the sparsely furnished rooms every time he picks up the receiver and dials. But now that his mother has grown accustomed to their rendezvous, she does not allow the phone to ring for more than a few seconds before she pounces on it.

When the tall, glass doors of the building are opened, he makes his way directly to the phone booths which line the wall of a room to the left of the main hall. He nods at the clerk on the front desk and is shown which cabin to enter. It is always the same clerk: a pale, ruddy man with a lisp who observes him with a mixture of distaste and curiosity.

Once inside the cabin, he closes the thin, glass door behind him and perches on the uncomfortable stool. Then he dials the number, with a conscious effort not to disturb his internal equilibrium with the competing forces of hope and despair. Today he is lucky, for after the first tone his mother's voice comes onto the line.

'Here I am,' she says immediately; the habit of talking on the phone never having replaced the immediacy of the language of everyday speech.

'How are you?'

'Fine, fine. You mustn't worry so much. I've been to the market already - there were apples today and dried figs.'

'Could you get all you needed?'

'You worry too much for a boy. I told you that I can look after myself.'

'I have to worry. I'm the only son and I left you there.'

Her voice changes now, compacts itself so that every tone seems to contain the force of her conviction,

'You know as well as I do that this is not your war. I will not have you killed for the sake of other people's ambitions, for ideas which we lived without for seventy years.'

He looks behind him as the adjacent cabin door is opened and a middle-aged man enters.

'Sssh. You mustn't speak like that.'

Through the bevelled glass he can make out the silhouette of the heavy figure as he searches in his jacket pocket to retrieve a piece of paper which he smooths out carefully before he starts to dial the number.

'They don't have time to listen anymore. There are more important things to worry about.'

'You never know,' he retaliates.

She pauses and he can see in his mind's eye her lip contracting in a desire to hold back the words she cannot allow herself to say to him.

'How is aunt Darya? The boys?'

'They are fine. Her husband is mostly at the front line but they get extra rations while he's there. She brought round a tin of molasses the other day.'

'What about the humanitarian parcels? Did you get one this week?'

73

'Yes, yes. I got my supply of dry beans and pasta.'

Her attempt at humour relaxes him a little and almost gratefully he lets out a short, dry laugh.

'Alma sends her love. We tried to call you on Sunday but...'

'Sunday morning it was bad...' she does not add the details and he does not ask her.

'You should have come, at least to Russia.'

It is the same line which he repeats, uselessly, every time he speaks to her.

'You know I couldn't have managed the journey. So many hours locked up in those trucks - my heart couldn't stand it.'

She has repeated this excuse so often that he is no longer sure if there is any truth left in it; if the weak state of her heart is a reality or a mutually accepted lie which hides her stubborn determination to remain at all costs in the house where she was born.

'I got a place at university.'

He has kept this news till last in order to save the conversation from its inevitable course of recriminations and regrets. All at once, her voice regains some of the joy he remembers from before.

'I can't believe it! I knew you would manage.'

Her unquestioning belief in the power of fate never fails to annoy him, and he rises up in defence of the effort it has taken him to reach his goal.

'It wasn't just a question of me, you know, there are rules and exams to pass.'

'Still, somehow I knew you would do it. Now you can at least have a future there.'

He laughs, sardonically, 'two more years of study, then I *might* be allowed the chance to apply for a visa to do a Masters or work in the university.'

'It is good news ...good news,' suddenly her voice is lost in a surge of static which pulses across the line.

'Need......paperwork.......engineering'
He calls her name a few times, conscious the whole time of the
body on the other side of the thin panel of glass.
'I can't hear you. I'll call next week.'
He annunciates the words into the silence which has replaced the
disturbance, unaware if she can still hear him.

Putting the phone down, he comes out of the cabin and pays the
bill that is waiting for him. He knows he should be satisfied that
he has shared his one piece of positive news with her but the
familiar feeling of disappointment is already settling inside him.

8

He has come to the club with the desire to see her again, though he has not admitted this to himself yet. As far as he is concerned, he only wants to find company for the night and this is where most of the youth from the centre comes at the weekends. Deliberately, he does not look over at the corner where he spoke to her last time but goes straight to the bar and orders a drink.

He has already spotted several people that he knows and they acknowledge each other with a brief nod of the head: a non-committal gesture which leaves each one free from the obligations of conversation if they want to avoid it. In such a small community, being alone in a crowd is a privilege granted to all men in deference to each other's need for privacy. Women on the other hand, especially attractive women, have to fight for the right.

It does not take long before he notices her sitting on one of the rare chairs that are scattered around the edge of the bar. Already, the incline of her head has become something intensely familiar to him and for some minutes he watches the way she is alone with herself. She emanates a calmness that lies like a neglected toy at the back of his memory; if he could manage for just one moment to penetrate that, he feels he would be able to recapture the peace of childhood sleep.

It is at the beckoning of her smile that he moves towards her, for he would not have had the courage to annihilate that moment. Clearing her jacket and bag from the ledge on the wall, she makes a space for him to sit down.
'Here again?'

He shrugs his shoulders, in a movement which encompasses both apology and indifference.

'Do you go to any other bars?'

His eyes flick towards her briefly, as if to check that the ground is ready for attack.

'I would go if you went there.'

There is no reason for his honesty, no premeditated plan of action which he has been working on during the sleepless hours of carly morning. There is just the hard core of an unyielding veracity, around which his soul is formed.

Her laugh is a poor attempt at diversion, leaving her on open terrain.

'Benjamin doesn't like to go anywhere to dance. He says he's nervous in crowds.'

Before the words reach her lips, they are a disappointment. He does not look at her in the eyes again, but speaks with his face turned slightly away. There is no sign of faltering in his voice.

'You get nervous of a crowd when you understand what people can do to each other.'

She turns her face away from him, uneasy with the sudden realisation that she doesn't really know who he is.

'Why did your grandparents leave Lithuania?' he continues, his desire for the truth unerring.

She looks at him for a long time without answering but when her voice comes out it is soft.

'It was the war. There was a toss up over who would take control – the Soviets or the Nazis: not much of a choice. So they got out.'

'You must to have a lot of money to leave?'

'My grandfather ran his own business, had lots of ties with the US.'

'I pay two thousand Euros to come across Russia.'

His eyes have become narrower, closed in on themselves, so that she cannot read what he is thinking.

'How did you come?'

'First by walking across the mountains. There were about ten of us, some people had a horse but I think they pay more. After we sometimes went by car but before the Russian border they were waiting with a truck. We got into the bottom part, under the floor and had to lie down, very quiet.'

'How long did it take?'

'Four days, I think. Maybe more, maybe less.'

'It must have been terrible.'

His voice is low and soft but in the split second it takes him to reply she can sense a hardening, a shutting down.

'It is not bad, only necessary,' he shifts his weight and carries on as if the two of them are discussing something quite banal, 'was it not hard for your grandfather to leave?'

'Of course it was hard - this was his home but in the end he decided it was the best thing to do.'

'But others stayed to fight.'

'It's a choice which is unique to each person and which no-one can judge. You should know that.'

Her attempt at revenge passes him by, for he is intent on knowing the facts and does not even notice its malice.

'Were they Jews?'

Clumsily, his tongue chooses the wrong word, with all its associated prejudice. Where he comes from they are nothing more than a legend of distant wars and hatred, yet his vocabulary is still tainted.

She was already in the process of standing when his question glanced across her mind and by the tension in her pose he can sense that she is wavering between turning round to face him or walking away. She is saved from the responsibility of decision by the appearance of two women coming towards her through the crowd.

He can tell immediately that they are locals (he knows the look so well by now and they are so proud of their round cheeks and pale skin) and watches their faces change to the hard mask of prejudice as they notice him. Momentarily confused, Lucy's face lights up again into a smile of unflustered self-confidence.

'These are my colleagues from work, let me introduce you…'

'But I know you,' interrupts one of the women: her face opening up in recognition.

Like an animal on guard, his shoulders rise in defence and there is downward jerk of the head as if the words that have somehow threatened his security. Lucy catches the movement and senses a danger she wouldn't even be able to explain but her friend continues, unaware,

'Don't you go to my university? I've seen you in the corridor…'

His eyes are still focused downwards and he does not audibly react to her words. This is one of the things that he fears; that one part of his life will slip carelessly into the other and the whole precarious balance will collapse. He tries extremely hard to keep the different components of his existence separate: his refugee life must not be allowed to intrude on his role as a student, nor is his family in any way connected to the people he spends his free-time with. And then there is the even more dangerous territory of the past life in his home country and the life he has now. All these are sovereign states whose integrity must not be questioned.

The tear in the fabric of convention unravels silently around the words that have gone unanswered, until finally Lucy reaches forward to gather the threads together,

'Ana teaches three days a week and studies for the rest of the time,' she tries to explain, 'do you have to pay for your studies, Ana, seeing as it is a second degree for you?'

Ana turns her face away from where it still stares at his: confused but yet not brave enough to step out of the game of manners.

'No, it's still virtually free, even for people like me who can't make up their minds,' she answers.

The three women laugh. He shifts his weight from one foot to the other.

'Let's dance,' suggests Lucy, with a sudden desire to escape the feeling of oppression which has come over her. The three of them move onto the dance floor, leaving him behind and he catches her eye only once as she finds her place in the crowd, before she is lost in the movement of bodies.

It is at this point that he knows he should turn and leave but instead he finds a place against the far wall and leans with his back against the graffitied concrete. The club is full of his countrymen tonight, as it is every weekend. They come here for that trace of what Lithuania and his homeland once had in common - the communist brotherhood which stretched from Eastern Europe to the far edges of the Soviet empire. Once they have cleared the street and entered into its windowless space there is a casual air of solidarity; an anachronistic world where the Russian Rock of their childhood is played alongside hip-hop.

This is what most of his people come here for; the comforting sense of equality which the place emanates. It is a perverted nostalgia, for they were never equal players in that artificial union, but sadness and loss have given them false memories, so that his people look back to that time with a longing for peace which is like a thirst for water. He can see some of them now, their bodies swaying to the beat of the music as if they each of them had a home to go to at the end of the night, as if tomorrow they would all get up to go to work or school just as they always have done.

And with a bitterness that has unexpectedly ruptured inside of him, he turns his gaze away from the place in the crowd where he knows she must be: if she came to him now, he would not be able to tolerate the unforgivable innocence of her presence. Is it a coincidence, he asks himself later, that at that moment he turned to see Zahra making her way towards him, or is it a sign of the way that things must be. She is not as fresh, nowhere near as vivid, as Lucy but she is one of his. He finishes the bottle of beer he is holding in one long swig and turns to smile at the face which is already glazed with perspiration.

'I didn't expect to find you here. I don't usually come to this place, but tonight it's Farhana's leaving party,' her words are part apology for what she fears he may see as some kind of infidelity.

'Where's she going?'

'To America,' she blushes and lowers her head as if she is embarrassed by her friend's desertion, and he takes her arm and moves her closer towards him.

'What do you want to drink?'

She asks for an orange juice but he brings her beer anyway and winks at her as he hands her the brown, glass bottle. He is not one for pretence; and when they first met she was already drunk.

She takes the drink from him and stands by his side as the two of them watch the people moving on the dance floor. Conscious of the eyes which may be watching him, he is robbed of the easy words which would usually fill the space between them.

'Are you tired?' she asks, finally.

He puts down his empty bottle and gestures to the exit and she follows him without discussion as he pushes his way to the door.

Outside, he gives her his hand unexpectedly and they walk towards the bus stop. He feels no discomfort in the absence of words between them, for he seems to have a confidence that she will follow where he leads without instruction. Walking along like this, he can almost believe that things are reforming themselves into the comfortable pattern of his old life. His memory is full of so many journeys home; coats zipped up to the neck, hands clasped inside his jacket pocket, impatient lips seeking each other. But Zahra is nothing like that other one, she is more pliable, more ready to listen than to talk. Perhaps that is why he chose her: for her ability to be silent.

When they near the bus stop, there are several teenagers from the centre already waiting and instinctively they pull apart. He greets them and offers around cigarettes while she keeps the distance which is expected of her. When the bus comes, the boys go straight to the back of the vehicle while the two of them find adjacent seats.

At night, when there is little traffic, it is only a twenty minute ride to the end of the line. Apart from them, there are only two local passengers who get out after three stops. The bus grinds on past the suburban buildings and the street lamps while the boys at the back sing and tease each other in their native tongue, and for a while it all seems so much like home. Only when they pull into the lay-by is the spell broken; the driver stepping out of his cabin with a gesture of irritated dismissal, waving his hand towards the doors and shouting 'Out!'

Walking very slowly, they let the group of boys overtake them then move close together again. The night is clear and now that they are away from the city lights they can see small wisps of white cloud moving across the stars.

When they are near the gates he takes her hand and pulls her close. Kissing her, he pushes his body tight against hers and feels her mould herself around him.
'Can you sleep with me tonight?'

He has been waiting for the moment to ask her, carefully timing it so that she does not have too long to consider the consequences.

'Don't you have roommates?'

'I have the key to where we were last time.'

She turns her face away, as if embarrassed to have to make a decision.

'Blacky isn't even there,' he whispers, 'he goes to the house where his mother works most weekends and leaves me the key.'

'I told my parents that we would all go with Farhana to the airport straight from the party …'

'Then you already have your alibi - they won't even miss you.'

Her eyes have widened at the hint of danger, and her body is caught in the immobility of indecision.

'If they found out…'

'If!' He blurts out, then changes tone and moves his head in very close to her, so that his lips are almost touching her ear. 'If we had all stayed at home we could be dead by now. But we are here.'

She nods almost imperceptibly and he leads her by the hand into the barrack. He is very gentle in his movements, opening the door quietly and locking it behind them. There in the dark, he is slower and more careful than last time, as if he is savouring every caress. When they have exhausted themselves, he turns to her on the narrow mattress and kisses her forehead.

'How come you managed to get here with both your parents?'

She raises her shoulders and lets them drop in a gesture of apology; having one's family together and safe in one place is a privilege which most do not have.

'By the time we reached the capital things had already become very dangerous – I think we took the last train out My father came too because he is crippled in one leg and couldn't fight,' she pauses as if waiting for him to respond but when he doesn't speak she continues, 'I thought we wouldn't make it. It seemed that the fighting was only a few hours behind us - every town we came to, by the evening we'd hear that fighting had broken out. We were almost clear, almost at the border when the train stopped dead in its tracks. We were made to get out – there were soldiers with rifles and civilians with pistols – some men they took away with them, others they pushed and abused. They could see my father wasn't a threat but they treated him with contempt, as if he was a coward for running away with the women. We were marched towards a bridge and kept waiting there for four hours. We couldn't go forwards or backwards. There were little kids with us, crying from thirst and hunger, but their mothers didn't dare to ask for water or bread. When they finally let us cross, I thought that my legs would cave-in beneath me.'

He sighs and reaches across her for his cigarettes. There was no accusation in her words, yet they rub the sore place of his conscience. It is not just a question of politics but of manhood and it is something he knows he must deal with for the rest of his life. 'You were lucky,' is all he manages to answer.

'My brother came out two months later. He couldn't stand being a soldier.'

He is reprieved – there will be no trail between them.

'Is he here? I don't remember...'

'No,' she answers, a little too quickly, 'he left almost as soon as he came - got a visa for Canada.'

'Canada,' he repeats uselessly: so many people have left that when the time comes for them to return home half of them will be missing.

She does not reply but watches the smoke as it leaves his mouth and disappears into the dark air. There is a lamp on outside the window and she can see his outline but not the expression on his face.

'You don't want to follow him?'
His words are hard and she feels a spasm of disappointment at their premature reference to the borders of their relationship.
'I want to go home,' she answers after a pause, 'not to some other place.'
'I know. And this is not even another place.' He laughs, almost to himself, 'this is just the in-between - the back door to Europe.'
He leans across her again to put out his cigarette, then tucks himself beneath the sheets.
'Let's get some rest; we should be out of here before light.'

***

It seems as if they have only been asleep for a matter of minutes when noises of confusion reach them from the corridor; the thumping and banging of doors, a desperate intake of breath and the whimper of someone crying. Zahra sits straight up in bed with a fear which comes from somewhere other than the present moment. He is also bolted into wakefulness and gets up immediately to dress.
'Don't go out,' she pleads, automatically.
The commotion outside has become more insistent. Ignoring her words, he pulls on his shirt and trousers, then turns to her and tells her to stay where she is.
Unlocking the door noiselessly, he steps out into the corridor. The lights have been turned on and there is a group of people at the far end bending over a limp shape on the floor. Stepping forward to see better, he feels his body pushed back by a hand which grabs him from behind.
'We need your help out here.'
He lets himself be led outside to where a group of men are circled around one man; some holding his arms as if restraining him, others talking and reasoning to his down-turned face.
'Leave her be, it can't be worth it.'

85

'You taught her a lesson, man, don't kill the woman.'
The man is no longer straining and it is difficult to make out the meaning behind the words which are tripping over themselves as they leave his mouth in one long stream of expletives.

'Where did you come from?' a voice at the side of him demands. It is Benjamin, shivering in T-shirt and gesturing for him to step away from the crowd.
'I was...' the question confuses him for a moment, 'what happened here?'
'Oh, the usual shit. Someone spread rumours about who looked at who, who spoke to who and the guy gets drunk and beats up his wife until she faints.'
'Fuck that,' he mutters, turning briefly to where the men are still negotiating, before heading back to his room. His own father died he was only six years old, so that he has no experience of the kind of discipline which husbands keep over their wives. He has no moral stance, no sense of outrage - just a simple distaste for the violence of the strong against the weak.

Benjamin follows him as he walks back to the barrack and the two of them enter to see women moving back and forth with bowls of water and tubes of ointment. There is the low chatter of excitement and fear.
'Come and help here,' one of the women, returning from the bathroom with fresh flannels, grabs his arm and tries to lead him down the corridor.
'What do you want me to do, woman?'
'You study medicine, don't you?'
He pulls her hand off his sleeve and turns away without responding.
'He's a student of Mechanical Engineering,' Benjamin's voice jumps in to explain.

'But she needs a doctor...' continues the woman, oblivious to her mistake.

'You can't call a doctor. Are you out of your mind?'

The man who has spoken is a member of the self-appointed resident's council: the liaison body between the management and the refugees. A minor government minister back home, his desire to serve those in power goes beyond any nationalistic sentiments.

'You get the doctor here and then you'll have the police,' he continues, his voice almost down to a whisper now 'and you know that they are just waiting for a chance to pin something like this on us.'

The woman doesn't answer but turns away in exasperation and enters into one of the rooms. The man moves towards to Benjamin, his tone conspiratorial.

'Go over to the B barrack and get the woman in room fifteen to come over here. She used to work as a dental nurse, she'll have to do.'

Obediently, Benjamin retreats through the door into the noisy darkness, leaving just the two of them alone in the sudden silence. The man looks at him as if he wishes to speak, to draw him into the intrigue of them against us, but he is too quick to turn away. He opens the door and disappears into the room before the words have time to lure him into unwanted responsibilities. When he enters he can see that Zahra is still sat upright in the bed, waiting for him to bring her the news.

'You can go to sleep,' he sighs, sitting down next to her in order to undress again.

She opens her mouth as if to ask what is going on but he catches the movement.

'Sleep,' he repeats, getting in beside her and rolling onto his side.

9

It is seven o'clock when the two of them awake and in the overlap between dream and reality he is confused as to which limbs belong to him, and which to Zahra. He shifts his left foot cautiously and nudges her into movement. Separating, he feels a brief pang of loneliness and watches her dark slim body move across the room with a hint of regret.

She dresses quickly, conscious of his eyes on her. Taking his watch from the table, where he placed it on top of his clothes, she lets out a gasp.
'It's late!'
He is amused by her sudden panic and for a moment he doesn't speak; watching the apprehension moving through her limbs.
'What are we going to do?' she continues, uncomfortable with his lack of reaction.
He sits up in bed and smiles.
'You could climb out the window.'
She looks at him, incredulous. Outside in the hallway the footsteps of the other inhabitants can be heard moving from room to room, while from the courtyard comes the shrieks of children playing.
'I'm serious,' he continues to look at her, testing her nerves.
She looks at the door as if trying to locate the exact positioning of the voices, weighing up the chances of getting out unnoticed. When she turns back to him, her expression has regained some of the bravado of youth which first made him notice her. She tucks her jumper into her trousers and buttons up her coat.
His face is not smiling but she can sense approval in his eyes. He gets up slowly and goes over to the window, pulls it open and checks outside for movement. Pulling a chair alongside the wall,

she comes up close to him, then pulls the hood of her jacket over her hair and lifts herself through the opening.

He does not watch her to check that she has passed by safely but goes back to the bed and lights a cigarette. As a man, there is no recrimination in his bringing a woman back with him, although there is always the threat of her family finding out. A few weeks ago he would never have dared to start an affair with someone from the centre, but the commencement of his studies has given him a sense of stability: for the first time since his arrival, he can see a future for himself here. He was even assured by the secretary of the Student's Union that he would be a priority for campus residence in his fourth year: a chance for a room of his own.

He looks around him as he inhales the bitter smoke: Blacky's room is smaller than his by half and is one of the rare rooms reserved for married couples. His mother must have bribed someone in administration in order to secure such luxury for her and her son, and she has tried to bring a kind of homeliness to the place by hanging small carpets on the walls and covering all the surfaces with hand-crocheted cloth. Now that she has secured a job in a private residence, Blacky has the benefit of comfort as well as the possibility to escape to a surrogate home life at the weekends. These privileges have caused a lot of jealousy amongst the other refugees, who have begun a sly campaign to get him into a communal room, thereby leaving this one free for those who 'deserve' it. But unlike the others, Blacky has a cash flow which will make this difficult to achieve; on top of his mother's earnings he takes ten Euro a night for the exclusive use of his room and bed. It is an arrangement which is quietly accepted but never publicly acknowledged – there are plenty of married couples who happily pay for a few hours of lovemaking away from the room they share with their parents and in-laws.

When he has finished the cigarette he gets up to dress himself. Half-heartedly, he pulls the bed covers straight before opening the door and locking it behind him. Two men speaking at the far end of the corridor turn briefly towards him, then back to their conversation. When he opens the door to his room, he can see Pale perched on the corner of his bed, consuming the maize porridge issued for breakfast from a plastic bowl resting on his knee. He looks up briefly from where his gaze is concentrated on the sticky, yellow mass and smiles a knowing smile – cocking his head slightly to one side in a gesture of congratulation. Although the two of them are from different ethnic groups and religions, they maintain a loose and easy relationship. Although he has never let Pale in too close, the two of them have an understanding which is based on a central self-interest and an inherent distrust of nationalism.

'Aren't you late for work?'
Pale gulps down the last spoon of his porridge and shakes his head,
'I managed to swindle the late shift today. First time in one year I get to sleep in.'
'It's a dog's life.'
'We can't all live the carefree student existence, you know.'
He picks up the pile of books and photocopies from his bed and waves them in Pale's direction.
'You call ploughing through this every evening easy?'
'You didn't seem to be doing much ploughing last night...perhaps you were sowing instead?'
He makes as if to throw the books in Pale's direction but then returns them to his bed.
'You missed breakfast. Take this.'
Pale gets up to leave and hands him a plastic bag full of bread: left-overs which the women in the kitchen give out at the end of every meal.

He takes a knife and a couple of catering packets of jam that he saved out of the humanitarian aid packages and carefully spreads the already hardening bread. When he has eaten three slices he clears the crumbs from his sheets into his hand, then throws them out of the window. The day is colourless and he is dismayed at the thought of having to stay a minute longer in the centre. Collecting together his books again, he puts them into his bag and takes his coat from the wardrobe.

As he opens his door, he sees the figure of Benjamin leaving his room and he waits for him at the exit so that they can walk together.
'Quite a night last night!' They are far enough away from the barracks for their conversation not to be heard, yet Benjamin's voice remains low.
'It's always the same shit. We don't need the Russians or the Americans or the army; we can destroy each other from the inside.'
Benjamin hesitates; he still has the conviction of youth 'You can't mean that. Our people have survived wars and invasions for thousands of years and still remained strong.'
He looks at him, amused, 'You believe too much of what the imams preach. What do you get to eat in that school of theirs?'
'What's that got to do with anything?'
'It's amazing what people will go along with when their bellies are full. What do they tell you - that the war is just another part of the global capitalist plot against the nations of Islam?'
'You think that's not true? Just look at the news – all the wars started or funded by the Americans are always against Muslims.'
'I think that each side has its own propaganda and its own sins.'
'You don't even believe what you're saying. Next thing you'll be reporting for CNN,' Benjamin thrusts a make-believe microphone beneath his friend's chin 'The growth of Islamic fanaticism amongst a disillusioned, unstable refugee population

can be seen in the growing numbers of religious schools which have risen up among the temporary collective centres across the former USSR, causing a threat to security in American embassies and military bases all over the region…'

Azad brushes his arm aside impatiently, 'Aren't you supposed to be studying for your lessons?'

Benjamin sighs, deflated, 'You know how it is. I can't stay cramped up in there all day. If my old lady tells me one more time about the cursed destiny of our people, I swear to god…..,' he pauses and shakes his head as if to rid himself of the annoyance. 'I'm going to meet up with some of the guys and play pool in Turk's pub. Want to come?'

'I can't, I've got to study before my lectures.'

'Just one hour, while there's nobody around. We can have the place to ourselves.'

He hesitates, weighing the options. The two of them climb up into the waiting bus and sprawl themselves on the empty back seats. They watch silently as two local people enter, glance briefly towards them, then sit down near the driver. The engine starts and there is a beeping noise to warn that the doors are closing, when the figure of Stony leaps through the closing gap.

'Shit, I nearly didn't make it!' he says, letting himself down theatrically into an adjacent seat.

'I thought you were already in town?' Benjamin asks.

'And I thought you were…weren't you supposed to stay at your girl's place last night?'

'Eh….'

'What's the matter Benjamin? Can't always make her give what you want?'

Benjamin raises his chin in a gesture of dismissal and makes as if to look out of the window.

'I saw her the other day at the club,' Stony continues, his hand nudging Benjamin's elbow where it rests on the back of the seat in front.

He shifts his weight uncomfortably. The image of Lucy flashes briefly across his mind; the hair on her forehead damp from perspiration.

'She's got quite some body on her. Don't say she doesn't know how to use it,' Stony taunts.

Benjamin's usually benevolent face takes on a look of superiority and he leans in closer towards Stony, lowering his voice to a whisper.

'I tell you what she is best at, something you'll never get out of our girls.'

'Say!' Stony's expression, as always, remains immobile but there is a tension in his body as he listens.

'Can't you guys do anything but talk shit all day long? There's a war going on and all you can do is gossip like school girls.'

His voice comes out sharp and disapproving and the suddenness of it takes them unawares.

'Whoa! Don't get all religious on us now - leave that to your holy roommate!' Stony barks.

'What's up with you?'

'Nothing's up with me. I just....'

Azad gets up, pushing roughly past Benjamin's legs and pressing the bell on the hand rail for the bus to stop.

'Where are you going?'

'I'm getting off here.'

'But this isn't your stop,' Benjamin protests.

Azad already has his back to them and doesn't bother to turn around to answer, 'I want to walk for a bit.'

The doors open nosily and he jumps out onto the pavement. As the vehicle moves past him, he sees Benjamin's bemused face search for his through the dirty glass.

***

Today, as usual, he leaves the lecture as soon as the professor has finished speaking, gathering his books under his arm and breaking out of the darkened room into the bright lights of the corridor.

He does not like to hang around after class, preferring to avoid any conversation outside of the collaborative work they must undertake as part of the course. From practice, he knows how to set up a protective wall of indifference around himself which allows him the freedom of anonymity. Older than his peers by at least five years, he likes to pride himself on the fact that he does not try to dominate nor to condescend.

Out on the street, the muted colours of dusk are already fading into the blackness of the early winter's evenings and the street is busy with people returning from work. The main road in front of the faculty is jammed with cars; impatient drivers ready to leap at the change of the traffic lights; their blank faces staring straight ahead, carefully avoiding eye-contact for fear of beggars. He steps off the pavement and weaves his way through them, feeling the heat from the engines as he passes near.

When he is in the middle of the four lanes the vehicles start to move around him, leaving him stranded until the next red light. On the pavement opposite, he notices a woman in a grey mackintosh pass by. It takes him a few seconds to recognise Lucy and the memory of the morning's conversation causes him to blush involuntarily. Without thinking, he raises his head to call to her, then stops himself short. Something in her posture dissuades him: a weariness in her gait, an expression of detachment which tells him that she wants to be left alone. Instead, he watches as she recedes into the distance, imagining her tiredness and boredom as she retraces the path she takes every day, taking out her key as she nears her door, throwing her coat and bag onto the nearest chair and sinking into the welcome seclusion of herself. When he can no longer make out her delicate form he steps off the pavement and runs to the other side of the road where the bus is waiting, its doors about to close. At this time of night, public transport is always full and he sits down on the only empty seat. His companion is an elderly man whose suit smells of tobacco and old sweat; his scrawny head nodding on his chest as he sleeps silently. Out of the window he watches the city recede and the dull, brick houses and apartments of the suburbs take over.

When the vehicle pulls in slowly to the final station, he gets up to leave, giving a nudge to the still sleeping figure of the old man. Jolting unexpectedly into consciousness, the old man's head jerks back involuntarily away from the dark skin of the foreign face in front of him.
'It's the last stop,' Azad annunciates, savouring the look of fear which focuses momentarily on him. The old man's eyes, narrow from tiredness, glance nervously through the window and then back. Almost unwillingly, he gives a nod of understanding; keeping his body very still as if in anticipation of some act of hostility.

Laughing to himself, Azad gets off the bus and starts to walk along the path towards the barracks with the men and women returning from the afternoon shift at the market; their bodies de-sexed in baggy tracksuits and overcoats, they trudge along in heavy boots and Wellingtons stained with earth from the vegetables they clean and pack all day. The few who catch his eye nod in greeting and one of them offers him a cigarette. He accepts it silently and pauses while the man lights it, then the two of them walk on in silence.

Outside the gate, the crowd disperses; disappearing behind the thin wooden doors and net curtains. Azad goes straight to his room and lies down on the bed, his coat and shoes still on. Before he has thought of taking them off, there is a knock.

'Come in!'

Benjamin opens the door and smiles nervously, then crosses the room to sit down on the bed. He seems embarrassed, like a child waiting to confess unfinished homework to his teacher. Taking a round biscuit tin from the plastic bag he is carrying, he opens the lid to reveal a selection of small, sticky pastries resting on patterned kitchen towel.

'My mother made them.'

Azad lets the inklings of a smile flash across his face and scoops one of the honey-covered pockets of pastry and nuts from the tin and straight into his mouth. 'They're good,' he says, when he has finally stopped chewing. He wipes his mouth with a cloth from his bedside cabinet and sighs. 'If it's about this morning, forget it. I was just in a bad mood.'

Benjamin's eyebrows knit together in an expression of incomprehension and then smooth out again in momentary relief. 'I already forgot about that. This is something else.....something difficult to...'

'Spit it out!'

'I've just been over in B barrack; things have been heating up over there all day....'

Azad looks at him blankly, not catching the gist of where the conversation is going.

'It's Zahra. Seems she stayed out all night and lied that she was at her girlfriend's leaving party. Her family have been going at her for hours to tell them the truth...I just wanted to warn you before...'

He lets out a short, intense laugh which seems at once genuine and without humour. It is as if he has finally received a letter which he has been expecting for a long time. More than a sense of indignation, he feels a gratefulness at Benjamin's quiet dependability – he must have known about Zahra for a while, yet has never mentioned it until now.

'What are you going to do?'

'Do?' he answers, as if amused by the idea. 'It's up to them now.'

'It's a matter of honour, you know - you didn't do it the proper way.' Benjamin's eyes are lowered, as if he is embarrassed at having to explain.

'It's the only way I know.'

The conversation is interrupted by the opening of the door, and Ismail enters the room, returning from his prayers. He eyes the two of them suspiciously, placing his rolled prayer mat carefully beside his bed. 'As sala'amu alaikum,' the words come out of his mouth like reproaches for a job not done.

'Walaikum as sala'am,' returns Benjamin.

Ismail nods as if he has won a concession then leaves them alone again, closing the door loudly behind him.

Benjamin turns towards Azad again, his eyes lit up with an untarnished earnestness, 'You know the rules. You should have asked for permission to start...'

'Whose rules: the Communists, the Lithuanians, the Prophet's?'

There is a pause, during which he picks up the cigarette packet from the bed. When he finds it is empty, he crushes the soft carton between his fingers and throws it across the room, then gets up and stares out of the window. Behind the barracks there is only waste ground, with a few spindly trees struggling to grow out of the barren earth. The soil is scattered with the over-flow of refuse which has seeped out of the centre and crept onto the surrounding territory: plastic bottles and cellophane wrapping; old clothes rejected from the Red Cross store; a stained mattress not fit even for refugees' use.

'If I was back at home...if all this hadn't happened, I would have graduated by now. Got married, had a kid maybe. How can they talk about rules when there are none left? When everything that we were taught…'he snorts in contempt 'the schools aren't even standing anymore. Talk about rules when there is no democracy, talk about God when there is no mercy, talk about hope when there is only survival.'

Benjamin shifts his weight self-consciously, watching his friend with an uncomprehending awe. There is the quivering of anticipation in the atmosphere, the kind of fused expectation that precedes violence. Outside the sky is heavy and grey, exerting an enormous pressure on the world below. Then suddenly, the air seems to relax and the anger fold back in on itself under the cover of propriety.
'What will you do?'
Azad turns back from the window but remains standing. The light coming from behind him obscures the expression on his face. 'Nothing. I've done nothing wrong, nothing which I have to defend. It's only love, after all.'
Benjamin smiles out of nervousness rather than relief: there is a coldness in his friend's tone which chills him.
There is another movement at the door and the two of them turn again to see the administrator of the night before, his head held high in a pose of exaggerated self-importance. His disapproving glance takes in the dishevelled beds and the debris of bachelorhood, before settling on them.
'You are expected in barrack B,' he pauses as if trying to remember his lines, then adds, 'room seven.' He does not wait for them to follow him but hurries out of the door, leaving it to swing noisily on its hinges before plunging the room into a wash of silence.
'Do you know what happened to the Jews of Vilnius?'
Benjamin's head jerks towards Azad in surprise, yet he does not answer.

'This city was once known as the Jerusalem of the north. Before the Nazis arrived, forty percent of the population was Jewish - now there's less than one percent. They're all buried out there somewhere,' he gestures towards the window, 'in the woods at Paneriai. Once they killed them, they burnt the bodies and then crushed their bones so that all traces of them would be erased.'

'How do you know all that?' Benjamin asks, afraid of the silence which has filled the room.

'There are plenty of articles on the Internet.'

'But didn't that happen all over Europe? What's it got to do with us?'

He comes towards the bed and leans his face in closer towards Benjamin's, so that his voice is almost a whisper.

'Perhaps that's what they want to do with us. The government, the Americans, the Europeans: crush us and bury us beneath our own soil and carry on as if we never existed.'

10

It is strangely silent inside the corridor of B barrack, as if everyone were constrained by the holding of breath; the tense expectation of punishment. He moves directly to the room which he has never entered, behind which are the seven square metres where Zahra and her family live out their lives.

He knocks and hears a sudden movement inside as a body lifts up its weight. When the door opens, he is faced with a man much older than he expected; deep lines cross the forehead and outline the large fleshy mouth and the hair has lost any of its previous colouring to a dull coating of metallic grey. Immediately, he takes in the worn, gray suit and frayed collar of the while shirt; the bias of the body towards the good leg; and he is touched with the same mixture of pity and revulsion he always feels when faced with inadequacy. The old man steps aside without comment and indicates for him to enter, then moves back to the bed, his left leg dragging unwillingly behind him.

Before he had entered, he had decided to avoid looking at Zahra during the interview, but now that he is inside his eyes are immediately drawn to her by the anomaly in her appearance. Instead of the bleached-blond hair, her face is enclosed in a dark brown headscarf which is tied tightly around her neck. Although his expression remains immobile as he looks at her, his body jerks at the shock and he is sure that he can sense her body retreat into itself in reciprocation. Of all the things that he had expected; anger, entreaty, pity, he had not counted on that: on the hard, unyielding rock of the base line.
Faltering only slightly, he manages to turn to the father,
'Respect to you,' he says, lowering his head in honour of his age.

The old man nods in return and indicates towards the chair which has been ostentatiously placed for him in front of the single bed.

Desperately avoiding the figure of Zahra, whose form he can just make out on the periphery of his vision, he takes in the tacky familiarity of his surroundings: the room itself seems to be separated into two sides – the old and the young. On the left there are posters of popular groups pinned to the whitewashed walls and a large class photo with a plastic spray of flowers attached to the upper, right hand corner. Underneath the photo there is a narrow, single bed identical to his except for the flowered bedcover and the worn, yellow teddy bear which rests on its pillow. The other side of the room, where the father has sat down next to his wife and daughter on the double bed, is hung with crocheted doyleys and bright, nylon prayer mats. Somehow avoiding the light which comes through the one central window, it seems the darker side.

The woman beside Zahra; whom he knows to be her mother, makes to get up then falters for a split second and looks at her husband. According to their customs, it is unheard of for a guest to arrive without being offered drink and food but the unsavoury circumstances have made her unsure. Imperceptibly, the old man nods: the dictates of hospitality are as binding here as back in their village. At his approval, the old woman moves towards the corner table on which there rests a small fridge, like the ones used for mini-bars in hotel rooms. Pulling out a carton of juice from inside, she prepares a glass for him and places it in on a small metal try along with a bowl of pistachio nuts and another of sunflower seeds. This she sets down tentatively on the bed behind him, then returns to her seat, her long skirts rustling with the movement of the body which remains anonymous beneath the layers of loose material.

He reaches for the glass and takes a first sip, then returns it to the tray. Opposite him, Zahra and her parents sit in silent, apprehensive formality; as if posing for a family portrait. The mother's features, he can now notice, resemble her daughters exactly except for the eyes. These she inherited from her father: the same wariness clouding the dark brown irises, behind which he can detect both hope and desperation.

'You know why we asked you here,' begins the old man, rubbing his hand along the thigh of his left leg as he talks. Patiently, he waits for a nod of recognition before he continues.
'It has come as a shock to us,' the old man's face makes a grimace as if the memory is painful and suddenly his voice reclaims the anger he feels he has the right to, 'it is against all our laws, our customs, to begin in this way. I know that you are from another part of the country, from the city, but to show no respect to us.....it is a very serious matter for a Muslim family.'
'Like you say, I come from the city; I wasn't brought up with the same customs.'

The old man is thrown by the neutrality of his words and there is a moment which is balanced between threat and negotiation, before his face regains its determination.
'We would like to know, before we make any final decisions, what your intentions are.'
Impulsively, Azad glances towards Zahra and catches her eye for the first time since entering. Strangely, the bare anonymity of the face unframed by the softness of her hair makes her seem much younger.
'You know what the punishment for such things is in our communities.'
At the sharpness of menace, he jolts with the sudden realisation of what this is really about. Growing up in a secular Soviet city so remote from the rural settlements where these people were

formed, he never once considered the risk to Zahra of actual harm.

'What exactly do you mean…?' his mind races faster than his voice and impulsively he shifts his weight as if to stand.

Hastily, her father raises his hand; his body flexed as if also to rise.

'Now that she has dishonoured us, if there is to be no suitable arrangement then we will have no choice but to renounce her and send her back. There are men at the front who need a wife.'

'Do you know what that would mean for her?'

'It is not my instinct but……' he flings his arm helplessly towards the door. 'We are not alone in having to make our decisions.'

'Do you people realise what century we are in?' his voice is low, concentrated into a tight ball of incomprehension and anger.

The father leans forward, 'these are desperate times: we have to maintain our integrity, keep our honour…'

His sentences have a habit of remaining unfinished; the dreadfulness of uncertainty hovering in their incompletion.

Out of the corner of his eye he notices Zahra's hand as it reaches across the expanse of space towards her mother, who pushes it away from her with a sharp movement. Looking at the mother and father now, he strains to detect the dreadful potential of revenge in their crumpled, worn-out forms. It is almost more than he can bear to have to watch the denouement of a tragedy played out within the hardboard walls and the cheap remnants of this temporary life.

'What is it you want from me?'

His words seem to provoke an unformed sigh of relief.

'The only way to save this situation is for you to be married,' the old man pauses, his hand still stroking the damaged part of his body, 'according to our laws.'

He looks up sharply, prepared to argue and yet something holds him back from comment; instinctively he understands that it is not these people, with their fear and their poverty, who are the real enemies. Zahra's eyes seem to have shrunk in on themselves in the wake of so much insistence: he was wrong when he thought she looked younger, for she is far older than anyone in the room.

'I do not have a job or even a homeland, as you know. I am a student of Mechanical Engineering in a country that does not want me.'

'You are educated; you come from a good family. An engineer can make a good living back home. When the war finishes...' the old man's voice is suddenly softened in the expectation of a satisfactory agreement.

'Yeah, when the war finishes.'

The two older people do not detect the irony in his words. There is more than years between them, there is the vast expanse of custom and education; lives so dissimilar that they could have been lived out it two different centuries.

'The imam has assured us that the ceremony would make everything proper; there would be no gossip or shame on us. But we must be quick, you understand.'

'I understand very well.'

Now that the threat has been made, there is no need for further explanation. He is aware of the cost of his indiscretion, the dreadful cost of trying to find some kind of comfort in this desert where they have been forced to take shelter. An extended silence stretches itself along the length of the room while each of them stares into the cavern of incomprehension which lies between them.

'Your father is alive?'

He shakes his head, 'He died when I was a child. My mother is still alive but she remained.'

'These are special circumstances, as we all know. We will not ask for a bride price.'

The old man pauses, as if he expects a gesture of gratefulness in the wavering of this archaic ritual. When he receives none, he continues falteringly,

'We cannot manage to do everything according to the book, but the imam has assured us...'

'I leave it to you to make the arrangements, according to your wishes.'

'I know my responsibilities. You will not be ashamed.'

Azad nods, his face neutral. Watching the two figures opposite he seems to see them as if through the wrong end of a telescope: their prematurely aged faces finally calmed by the knowledge that they have not trespassed across the borders which contain their world.

'You have not told me how we will live.'

The father looks at him, uncomprehending.

'I share my room with two other men. It is not the place for a married couple.'

The mention of sleeping arrangements has made the old man nervous; he is again filled with suspicions and anxiety as to what has gone on before. There can be no way of knowing what Zahra told him and what he has surmised for himself. For the first time in the conversation he glances at the stiff, unrelenting figure of his wife.

'Everything can be arranged, I am sure. There are married rooms, as you know. I will ask the imam, he will take care of everything.'

He is dismayed and amused at their belief in the powers of the retired cleric, whose once upright figure is now bowed with age. The atmosphere in the room, now that the situation has come to a satisfactory conclusion, is one of sudden embarrassment, as if they had all simultaneously realised themselves for what they are: strangers grasping for order in a foreign place.

'I will leave you now. Send for me when you have made the arrangements.'

Rising from the cold, metal chair he sees the two old people share a quick, furtive glance.

'You will not be allowed to meet Zahra again before the day. That is the way it has to be.'

He looks over at Zahra but her eyes are fixed on the ground in front of her. Instead of the sense of outrage he expected, he feels an overwhelming sense of pity which is inexplicitly tinged with relief.

'Of course,' he answers and holds out his hand to grasp the old man's: his skin is hot and dry.

***

The corridor is still hushed when he exits and as he moves he can feel the stares of those who are gathered about the steps or at their windows. Outside, he is struck by the freshness of the air after the stuffy intimacy of the Zahra's room.

In front of his own barrack he can see the figure of Benjamin crouched by the edge of the pitch, his hands busy with a piece of chalk on the dark asphalt. He looks up as he approaches, his eyes narrow with concern, waiting for news.

'What happened?'

He looks at him for a few moments, then squats down beside him on the gravel verge.

'It was all very amicable - just a touch of blackmail.'

'What do you mean?'

'You know what I mean. You must know the rules of the village far better than I do; the cost of unsanctified love. They threatened to send her back home, to force her into an arranged marriage.'

Benjamin's eyes jerk quickly towards the barrack and then back again, his eyelids twitching as his mind races to fill in the details.

'You must be kidding me. They're not that kind of family…' His voice loses its power and he turns once again to look at the squat, grey building opposite. 'She doesn't even wear a veil.'

'She does now.'

Benjamin's eyes fall to the ground in front of him, as if searching for an explanation in the white scratches which his hands have drawn on the black surface.

'It's the way things are now. They can't be like they were before. The war has taken away our freedom to be what we want to be.'

Azad looks at his friend's head, bent under the weight of disbelief and lets out a low, short laugh.

Benjamin looks up, concerned,

'What's there to laugh about?'

'Is it not funny? The thought of me saying my marriage vows in front of the imam, my future wife piously enclosed in a veil.'

'You are going to marry her?'

'You think I have a choice? Marry her or they will make sure, in one way or another, that she will not be able to shame them again. How do you think that they treat soiled goods on the front line?'

'You can't be serious that they would send her back…'

Benjamin's eyes search the horizon, then fall back to the ground in front of him: it is as if he cannot bear to look at his friend's face, as if he too is complicit in their guilt.

'Have you heard what some women back home do in order to get out of arranged marriages? They douse their clothes in paraffin and set themselves alight.'

He looks at Benjamin, searching for a reaction, watching the curve of his back rising and falling.

'I didn't know it would go so far. I should have warned you.'

'Warned me of my own people?'

Benjamin shrugs and turns to look at him, 'can you manage?'

Azad looks away, past the faded facades and beyond the green line of the distance but his eyes do not see anything. Internally, there is a movement in his brain, as if a sagging weight has been transferred to another, deeper level, leaving only cold vacant air in the wake of its departure.

'If one cannot go through with something, one shouldn't start it.'

'Is this what you wanted?'

Unexpectedly, it is anger that has suddenly rushed to fill the space left inside him.

'Does it seem like that to you? That I wanted a family almost torn apart, another group of individuals forced into submission by fear and ignorance?'

'I only meant…'

'What? Good will? God's Will? Don't you really feel, at the end of the day, that this is the right thing to do? You can sleep with foreign women, but Muslim ones are for marrying. Aren't these the morals they teach you in that school of yours?'

Benjamin starts, offended by the spite in his words, 'You know I don't think like that. But you two could be happy together - sometimes it is better like this, when fate pushes your hand.'

He laughs, 'You are like the Russians; they also have their faith in *sudba*.'

'We have our own word for it,' Benjamin looks at him now, a spark of defence in his blue eyes.

'I'm sure you do but you forget - in the city we were taught Russian.'

11

He feels a wave of relief pass through him when he realises that it is Sunday morning and that he has managed to sleep straight through the night for the first time in months. Glancing over at the clock, he smiles in surprise at the hands resting contentedly on eight. Propping himself up on his elbow, he lights the last cigarette from the packet next to his bed. The smoke leaves his mouth in perfect, quivering circles, then collides with the sunlight coming in through the window and disperses in a bluish haze.

It is one of those rare mornings when he has the place to himself and can survey his situation with the clarity of thought which only thrives in solitude. The constant presence of other people: their voices, their movements, their imprints on everything around him, leave no space for reflection. It is at moments like these, in the lull of human activity, when the fear usually seeps through the seams of his self-control. Yet today there is a stillness inside him; a feeling of absence like the aftermath of death. The room, crammed full with the debris of three lives up-rooted, seems shabby and temporary in the bright light. Yet he has no proprietary feelings; there is even a deliberate lack of personal investment in his surroundings as if the addition of any decoration, any item of luxury, would indicate a state of undesired permanence. Some of the families in the centre have hung curtains at the windows, placed plants on the sill, but for him this would be capitulation.

Stubbing out the cigarette in the over-full ashtray, he gathers together the things he needs for the day. There is a slight sensation of agitation inside him at the promise of escape; albeit to the temporary shelter of Alma's carpeted home. Perhaps he will tell her the news of his engagement; just for the pleasure of seeing her features tighten into the slightly envious incredulity he expects she will display. He knows that all women feel a sense of possession towards every man in their lives; an unwillingness to let them be taken care of by another female. Alma has always been like an older sister to him, despite the efforts by her husband to keep them apart.

Once his bag is full of this week's washing, he retrieves his coat from the tightly packed wardrobe, then carefully takes the hat from the pocket and puts it on. Outside, there is a chill wind which seems to rise up from the earth and dislodge forgotten piles of leaves and refuse left over from autumn. All at once, it stirs a kind of restlessness in him which makes him uneasy. Winter has left the courtyard deserted and the only sound to be heard is the combined drone from the television sets that stay switched on every waking hour of the day.

As if the cold has amplified the acoustics of the morning, his footsteps grate through the gravel, then clatter on the asphalt of the main road. His coat is buttoned up to the limit but still the chill of the wind manages to seep inside him. He has not seen a single soul since waking up and he realises that this has never happened before during his entire stay in the camp. He has the odd sensation that during that long blank sleep, the inhabitants of the earth have somehow evaporated and only he has been overlooked.

When the bus arrives, it is one of the old vehicles which have not yet been decommissioned; a rusty blue hulk with steep steps up into an interior devoid of comfort. In concession to the weather, the driver opens the doors to let him wait inside until the scheduled departure and he sits down on one of the cold, metal seats, feeling the vibration of the ageing engine run through his legs. Out of the window, the frigid air outside seems to have bleached the landscape to a pale display of muted shades, foretelling the imminent anonymity of snow.

When he arrives at Alma's he finds the door is left open as usual although there is no greeting when he enters the empty hall. He does not take off his coat, for there is a feeling of concentrated apprehension which draws him directly into the living room. Unusually, he finds Thomas seated in the armchair, his back to him as he watches the television, while Alma is standing beside him, her hand resting on the worn fabric of the seat. There is something about the position of her hand, the tension of the limb so obviously not at rest, which makes him uneasy. And when she turns to him, he can see that his intuition is not mistaken.

'What's wrong?'
He speaks in Lithuanian, out of deference to Thomas and his voice sounds strangely loud and present against the muted tones of the TV.
Alma's look is hard, uncomprehending, then softens as she understands that he is not aware of what has happened.
'It seems there was a big offensive during the night. They took the capital.'
He moves forward instinctively, seeking the images which will confirm her words, but on the screen he can see only the Lithuanian President stepping off a plane to be greeted by a party of military officials: the story has already moved on.
'What did they say?'
'There wasn't any detailed explanation. They must have started the offensive just after midnight. We only heard when we turned the radio on this morning and by then it seems it was all over. They had no chance...'

Her voice dies off as she watches Thomas getting up suddenly from the armchair and turn to confront him.

'If there were enough people to defend her she wouldn't have fallen!'

Alma turns to follow her husband, her arm flung out behind her in a wild gesture of appeasement towards where he is standing. Following Thomas, he moves towards the hallway where the three of them now stand, squashed together between two narrow walls.

'What do you mean by that?' he almost shouts.

'You know what I mean.'

Thomas already has his coat on and his eyes are concentrated on the buttons which he is fastening with feigned concentration.

'Thomas, please, it's not the time to talk about that.'

Her hand goes out to his turning back and falls uselessly through the air.

'What the fuck do you know about it? About war, about holding a gun and being told to shoot or be shot.......'

The words fly at the closing door, which bangs shut and leaves the two of them standing, uselessly, like people who have missed their train. In the quiet that follows, she seeks his gaze but he turns away from her, running his hand through his thin hair as if suddenly finding himself lost in a strange place.

'He didn't mean it.'

There is a twitch of the head, as if he is avoiding a blow but he does not speak. She moves forward and again her hand reaches out for something which has already moved away. Her arm flutters indecisively in the air between them, then drops down ineffectually at her side.

He picks up his bag and flings it onto the chair where Thomas was sitting and she picks it up immediately, like a token of peace and automatically walks towards the bathroom. Unexpectedly he does not follow her and as she turns round to look at him, she is shocked to see the paleness of his face.

'You're not going?'

'I can't stay now.'

Looking around her, as if for an anchor for her words, she surveys the empty living room: the TV still flickering and droning in the corner, the untidy cushions of the just-vacated seats.

'I wish you wouldn't.'

He looks at her for what seems like a long time but does not speak, then pushes past her and out the front door. She hears the catch fall and a few seconds later the hum of the lift descending.

***

Outside, the wind has subsided, leaving in its wake a feeling of emptiness. Deliberately, he crosses the street to avoid the sunlight which falls off the roofs of the buildings and illuminates the pavement, watching his shadow melt into the shade cast from the trees in the adjacent field. A voice inside his head is counting out the steps as he walks: his only intent to get away from the centre and Alma's flat and every place where he is known; to be anonymous amongst the architecture and the traffic. His mind is filled with an indignity which ruptures with a slow heat inside of him.

Walking for the sake of movement, he avoids the busy main boulevards and takes the dull, straight side roads with their crumbling socialist apartment blocks punctuated by strips of land filled with rusting swings and slides. The large metal bins which line each driveway are already bulging with the weekend refuse, attracting the ubiquitous stray cats; their air of superior indifference unruffled by the greasy state of their fur and the crusted scars which mark their heads and necks. There are few people out this morning and those that do walk along the neglected streets are thoughtful and silent, as if out of respect for the demise of an obscure distant city, once part of a willingly forgotten empire.

The shabby urban landscape seems to go on for ever, unchanging in its poverty of colour and style: an endless display of peeling paint and twisted iron fences, uneven pavements and the detritus of neglect gathered in the gutters and the corners of unkempt gardens. It is only on the border of the old town that the world becomes a safe and sanitary place again, and he walks onto the immaculate main street like a trespasser on private property, taking in the gentle sweep of the newly laid cobbles which lead to the cathedral, framed in green by the hill which rises behind. Passing by the main square, he crosses the bridge and pauses for a moment to look down at the river which curves obediently through stone embankments. The winter sun, muted silver, flickers across the water and bleaches pale the green of the leaves which still remain on the trees. He has never been to this part of town before, to where the shops and bars end and give way to the green of gardens and the boxed town houses with their faded pastel-coloured facades. Already, his mind has started the process of understanding; repeating the words that were said between himself and Tomas and Alma, interpreting every look and gesture.

It is only at the corner of his consciousness that he notices a familiar voice calling him from nearby. Distractedly, he moves his gaze from the water towards the sound, and sees the figure of Lucy approaching him. At once he takes in her red jacket, the tightness of her dark jeans, the hair just recently brushed: unintentionally, his lips form the beginning of smile.

Without speaking, he leans forward to take one of the plastic bags she is carrying but the gesture takes her unawares and she takes a step back.

Amused, he smiles and explains, 'I want to help you carry them.'

Blushing, she releases the handles into his hand and looks down briefly at her reddened fingers.

'Where do you live?' he asks, almost carelessly.

She gestures with her head to the other side of the road and the two of them step off the pavement to cross.

'I had to go and get some supplies,' she explains, feeling obliged to justify herself despite the fact that it is he who is out of place here, 'I don't seem to have time during the week.'

'I thought there were no shops open on Sundays.'

'There's a twenty-four hour store just round the corner.'

'Oh yes, I forgot, this is Europe - Capitalism first, religion second,' he jokes, watching the fine line of her cheekbones as she smiles in response.

Her flat is on the ground floor of a two-storey house, shielded from the road by a screen of tall, evergreen bushes. He watches as she searches in her jacket for the key, then opens a door that leads straight into a kitchen.

Putting the baggage down on the large, wooden table, he notices the silence.

'Your flatmate?'

'Oh,' she hesitates, as if suddenly aware that the two of them are alone, 'she's gone to the U.S. for two weeks - her sister had a baby.'

He does not answer her but looks around him, slowly taking in his surroundings: the table scattered with boxes of cereal and packets of biscuits; the sink full of crockery waiting to be washed; the row of plates stacked on the draining board. Only the stove seems clean and he has the impression that it is rarely used. It is the kitchen of a Western woman, he thinks to himself: a passing through place.

Uncomfortably, she notices his look of disapproval, 'We're not often here,' she explains, 'there's a canteen at the school and otherwise, well you know - pizza, sandwiches...Do you want some coffee?'

He nods and she gestures towards the adjoining room, accessible through wide double doors.

'Sit down. Make yourself at home, as we say.'

Laughing nervously, she turns towards the cupboard and searches for the cups.

In the living room there is the minimum of furniture: a low table and a shelf on which there are a few paperback novels, some dictionaries and books on English grammar. He takes off his coat and sits down on a wide sofa which he realises must also double for a bed, for there is a wardrobe in the far corner. Beyond the door at the other end he can see a short hallway leading into a bedroom. He clears the table of the magazines and sets them down on the far end of the sofa. He can hear Lucy's movements in the background as she prepares the coffee and he has already decided what he will do.

'Where do you sleep?'

She blushes as she sets the cups down on the table.

'We drew straws: I lost, so Emma got the bedroom and I sleep here.'

He takes the cup and stirs in a spoonful of sugar. His hands are thin, the veins very visible along his slim fingers. She moves a chair from by the window and sits down on the other side of the table.

'You make good coffee.'

'I learnt here. We drink filtered coffee at home but Ben...' she falters at the name, then tries to carry on as if nothing has happened 'Benjamin taught me this way. I always drink it like this now.'

He shows no indication that the mention of his friend has made him uncomfortable; his face is implacable as he listens to her comments.

'In America we drink this kind of black water by the galloon. I was never a big fan of coffee but since coming here....well, so much about me has changed since coming here...'

Her words fall away into silence and for a few seconds she tries to avoid his stare as she searches her mind for something to say.

'I am sorry if I insult you last time.'

She falters, unsure of what he is referring to.

'Asking if you are Jewish ...it is not my business.'

She sighs, her face taking on a look he has not seen on her before but which he recognises so well: a kind of cynical acceptance of man's prejudice, of the extent to which people are prepared to hate.

'In Europe it seems that it's everybody's business.'

'My family were communists. I have never been in a Mosque but I am Muslim to everyone here.'

'Then you know what it's like.'

'For us it is a question of culture in the end. When communism went, people look for what feels safe, to what feels like their way of life. Suddenly it's as if those seventy years mean nothing to us.'

'It's too easy to cling to doctrine rather than make up your own mind.'

He smiles, indulgently 'We do not come from a country with a history of freedom, we do not see ourselves as individuals like you do.'

'Do you speak for all of you?'

'You have to be careful, that's all. You take us like you do people from your home but with us it is different. We are a tribe

117

and now we are a tribe at war. We cannot be separate from our culture; in the end we are prisoners to it.'

'Is that a warning?'

Surprised, she secs him hesitate for the first time; the seconds of silence filling up with the voices of those who are not present. The tension is broken by the ringing of the telephone and she jumps up a little too quickly to search for her mobile amongst the shopping bags on the kitchen table.

'Hello?'

There is a silence while she listens and then her voice crouches into a whisper so that he cannot tell what she is saying. He gets up and opens the door of the wardrobe; inside there are a couple of dresses and a long, winter coat hung loosely on hangers and a pile of trousers and jumpers bundled at the bottom. He closes the door and moves towards the kitchen.

Placing the phone back on the table, she turns to face him as he walks towards her. She has enough time to notice her own lack of surprise when she feels his mouth on hers; his rough stubble rubbing against her cheek. There is the force of desire in his hands and lips and yet his touch is light, almost tender. The memory of it has stayed with her since that day at the bus stop and she knows herself well enough to understand that this is what she has wanted all along.

His thin body is hard and unyielding against hers and suddenly, feeling herself falling, she tries to pull back. 'I shouldn't...'

Brusquely, he completes the gesture; holding her head in his hands so that she is forced to look in his eyes.

'You have to do something or not do it. You can't be in the middle with your guilt.'

There is a brief pause, in which they both realise that the decision has already passed them by. He lets his fingers run gently down her cheek as his hands drop to his sides.

'I'm sorry; I can't do that to him.'

'It's not just about sex.' His head is already turned away from her but the words are clear. His tone is neutral, like a teacher explaining a theory he has repeated so many times.

She lets out a sigh in the attempt to expel the taste of disappointment from her mouth. 'You don't have to go.'

'The capital fell last night.'

His words come as a surprise; moving so abruptly from the intimate domain of the two of them to the dangerous expanse of the outside world. Even through his shirt, she can notice the tension in his back as he leans down to gather his coat from the sofa.

'I...I didn't know. I haven't watched the news today.'

Turning slowly towards her, she can detect reproach in his eyes.

'You don't have to,' his shoulders rise and fall in an exaggerated shrug.

'Do you have anybody there?'

She regrets the words before they are out of her mouth, watching his lips form themselves into a kind of grimace.

'Does that matter?'

Without answering, she lowers her eyes like a schoolgirl told off for talking in class. There is a moment when he comes very close to her, when she can almost feel the fabric of his clothes brush against her side and then he is gone: already standing in the kitchen to put on his heavy coat.

'You should call Benjamin. He has family there, I think.'

His face is hard, his movements stiff and precise. She nods in response and watches as he fastens the last button and turns to leave.

12

The journey back to the centre of town is not one which he performs with his conscious mind. Like a sleep walker, he goes through the motions of walking, breathing, checking for traffic, while in his head he exists in another time and place. Images of his home flit randomly across his mind; his desk in the corner of his childhood bedroom, piled with papers and files and books loaned from the library; the large tiled kitchen where they ate their meals; the disgruntled face of the woman who came to clean and cook twice a week: a practice left over from the more affluent days when his father was alive and never discontinued. He can see everything perfectly clearly, even down to the scratches on the walls and the squeaks of certain doors which had never been oiled and yet he cannot call up the image of his mother. He has become accustomed to this phenomenon, for ever since he left her he has been unable to reproduce her features through an act of his own will. It is only in moments of dream or half-awareness that her image will form itself for him, diluting itself into caricature the moment he tries to capture it. After only twelve months absence, he is left with the poorest of memories; only the hard unrelenting reality of objects manage to reproduce themselves in his mind.

Without thinking, he stops himself short at the bus stop and takes the first vehicle that comes. It is one of the ancient trolley buses still in use despite its rusted exterior and the hard, inadequate seats bolted to the filthy black floor. He notices when he enters the frill of a narrow strip of curtain that the driver has pinned across the windscreen, below which there hangs a photo of a woman and a child: a clumsy gesture of homeliness.

He has not been more than a few minutes on the dilapidated vehicle when it stops suddenly at an unmarked stop and he notices the dark grey uniform of the ticket inspector enter. Moving at a steady pace through the crowd, the inspector makes his way down the line of seats, silently holding out his hand towards each passenger in a ritual of humiliation which he seems to relish.

Azad knows that he has two choices: to try to make his way to the back of the bus and escape via the rear door at the next stop, or to stay where he is and bluff it out. Unconsciously, he feels the quickening of desire at the thought of confrontation.

'Ticket!' The inspector's face is large, his features stretched flat across it.

He hands over a ticket from the bunch he keeps in his wallet.

'But this has not been validated.'

'I forgot,' Azad's expression is blank, liberated by the freedom of knowing he has nothing to lose.

'Give me your ID!'

'I don't have one.'

'Every Lithuanian citizen must carry their ID with them at all times. To leave home without it is a criminal offence.'

'I am not a Lithuanian citizen.'

'What is your occupation here?'

'Refugee.'

The man lets out a snigger through his wide nose, 'That is not an occupation.'

'It is all I am allowed to be in the Republic of Lithuania.'

The inspector turns and lets his eyes briefly scan the area around him. Nobody has visibly turned to look at them and yet he feels the stares of every other passenger waiting for his response. There is the prickle of accusation in the air, as if the bus were suddenly charged with static electricity. His eyeballs still shifting in their sockets nervously, he flicks his head back and moves between the crowd. After a few seconds he returns, holding his stamped ticket in his hand and passing it to him in a gesture of dismissal. 'One ride, one ticket!' he barks, then moves on down the line, his quick, efficient fingers retrieving and returning tickets to the out-stretched hands that wait for him.

Azad feels no sense of victory in the retreat, yet in spite of himself he experiences a feeling of disappointment; a brief concession to a fundamental part of him that longs for the neatness of violence. Imprisoned too long in confined spaces, there is an unacknowledged yearning inside him for the wide domain of the physical: the chase, the adrenaline, the oblivion of pain.

When the vehicle jolts to a halt back in the west of the city, he thrusts his way towards the doors and manages to extract himself before the metal panels close with a loud hiss. He turns briefly to consider the wide empty street before crossing to the other side, so impatient for movement that he doesn't consider waiting for the bus home. The sun is low in the sky now and there are more pedestrians than in the morning; people walking dogs or accompanying their relatives home after a family lunch. He passes them without causing any unwanted attention, for in this part of the city his dark skin is less uncommon.

When he arrives back at the barracks the suffused blue light of evening is already creeping into the crevices between the trees. The place is as empty as when he left it: silent in the aftermath of defeat as if the terrible imaginations of all those inhabitants have forced them into hushed submission. He has no desire to meet anyone, to share the inadequate grievings of the women and children and feel again the burden of his own betrayal. Cutting back on himself and circumventing the main gate, he ducks into the bushes and skirts around the wire-mesh fence until he reaches a jagged hole cut out for the benefit of those who wish to enter and leave unnoticed by the guard. The divided metal opens up just outside his room, allowing him to enter through the window if there is a willing accomplice on the other side. Cautiously, he draws his face close to the dusty glass and peers into the unlit interior. He can just make out the contours of Pale's immobile body lying on the bed and tentatively he knocks on the flimsy pane.

Pale twists his head around towards the noise, grimaces and then gets up slowly to open the window.
'What have you done wrong?' his voice is groggy from sleep and he flops back onto the mattress without waiting for an answer and closes his eyes again.
'Just didn't want to have to speak to anyone,' Azad replies, balancing on the sill and throwing himself adroitly into the room.

Once inside, his eyes instinctively register something significant and immediately he focuses on a small, brown packet resting on the pillow of his bed. It has no address or postal marks on its smooth surface and he hesitates before picking it up.
'Where did this come from?' he does not turn around as he says this and his words do not reach the already unconscious mind of Pale.

Something hard and heavy slides to the bottom of the envelope as he handles it and slipping his hand into the padded cellophane interior his fingers grasp a heavy solid object. Glancing briefly over his shoulder at the supine figure, he notices a hot wave of uneasiness break across his skin as his hand falters for a spit second. When he pulls the object out, he is almost relieved to see the oblong form and the metallic buttons of a mobile phone. Although the model is from a few years back, it is unused, with the small protective square of polythene still covering its screen. Cautiously, yet with an unsolicited sense of satisfaction, he feels the pleasing weight of it rest in the palm of his hand. With a flick of his index finger, he switches it on and watches the display light up in a spurt of colour. Scrolling through the buttons he can see that there is one number in-putted, listed simply under the letter A. He looks at it long enough to realise that it has an international code, then presses the top switch again and swiftly throws the phone back on the bed.

Behind him he is acutely aware of the regular rise and fall of Pale's breathing, while beyond the wooden door he can hear the shuffle and murmur of life as usual. Inexplicably, he senses that he must make a decision quickly, before the noises become too much to bear. All his life he has instinctively avoided anything which tried to deprive him of his freedom; any hint of radicalism. If his father had remained alive, there would have inevitably come a point when they would have disagreed on matters of communist doctrine which infringed on the dignity of the self. Yet there is a wrinkle in the fabric of his conscience, a tiny fault-line of desperation which inhibits the process of choice. Bending forwards, he picks up the phone and gently places it back in its packet, carefully folding the opening to keep it tightly enclosed. Then he lifts up the corner of his mattress and thrusts the envelope as far as he can up against the wall.

***

Lying in the half-light of evening, he opens his eyes to the blank, white ceiling without a memory of anything other than the knowledge of his own self. Like an amnesiac, he has to consciously remind himself of the ever-narrowing circles of his recent history, right down to the present moment and the realisation of where he is: the war, the escape, the refugee centre, the cramped room and the identity of the other body sleeping beside him. Without his bidding, the pale face of Lucy arranges itself before him and then the sad eyes of Zahra when he last saw her, seated beside her implacable mother.

Cautiously, he swings his legs off the side of the bed and lifts himself up, not wanting to wake up his sleeping roommate in the process. He has no idea if Pale noticed the small envelope which now rests uncomfortably beneath his mattress, yet he is sure that the person who left it would not have let himself be seen. Instinctively, his eyes flit across the room to Ismail's bed but it is smooth and empty; untouched since the early morning when he left for prayers. He turns to take his cigarettes and his coat from where he threw them on the cabinet and steps quietly out of the room.

The corridor is empty; its rumpled vinyl floor poorly illuminated by the three bulbs which hang along the length of it. He closes his door gently and crosses over to Benjamin's room, knocking lightly in case his family are sleeping. After a few seconds of shuffling and the rustle of plastic bags, Benjamin peers out at him and smiles. The room is dark except for the intermittent flickering of unnatural light coming from the television that is placed on a cabinet under the window. Briefly, his eyes catch the dark green of uniforms and the muffled sounds of explosions. The seated figures of Benjamin's mother and sister do not react to the intrusion, their bodies tense from sustained vigilance.

'You want to come for a walk?'
His words come out trivial and at the same time heavy with significance, as if the need to flee and to remain are two equal partners; both imperative and ridiculously useless at the same time. Yet it seems to him that the expression that appears on Benjamin's face is one of gratitude and without hesitation he

reaches behind the door to take his jacket, then follows him into the corridor.

'You don't feel well?' Benjamin asks.

'No, I'm alright. I just wanted some fresh air.'

He steps out first into the chill of the evening and Benjamin follows him. Across the courtyard, there is a sudden agitation and the briefly glimpsed colours of skirts and scarves. The movement is quick and undefined but is noticed by both of them.

'Have you seen Zahra since then?'

Azad does not respond; his concentration fixed on the closing door.

'I spoke to some of the girls from her corridor. They said the situation had calmed down and that the parents are announcing the marriage as if there were nothing out of the ordinary. They were even boasting about the fact that you were an engineer. They have you graduated already!'

He smiles unwillingly, then turns away and lets his eyes run over Benjamin's smooth face.

'Do you remember the first day you came here?'

'To the centre?'

Azad nods, his gaze moving away and skimming the so-familiar surfaces; the dark brown wood, the rough concrete and the grey, uneven asphalt. 'I came at the end of summer. It was already chilly and the leaves had started to turn. There were three of us in the van, transferred from the police station: Ismail, me and Pale. I don't think we spoke to each other the whole ride.'

'Why were you in the cells?'

'We had all come illegally over the border, in one way or another - that's crime enough.'

'We already came the year before – there were still convoys out then. Our bus was organised by the Red Cross for women and children. When we finally got here there was hot soup and clothes parcels waiting for us.'

He does not answer and in the silence their own footsteps fall nosily on the gravel path. It is dark and there is no moon, so that they can barely see each other's faces.

'Did you hear anything from your relatives?' Azad asks at last.

'We were calling all day. Most of the wires are down, I suppose, but we managed to get through to a neighbour - some kind of relative I think. Everything is calm for now. There's a curfew, so nobody has been able to see what's going on. They told us there was still gunfire in the morning but now it's all quiet.'

'Maybe gunfire is better. I distrust the silence even more.'

Benjamin lets out a low, extended noise but does not answer. The air is cool and he stops briefly to zip up his jacket.

'Do you think one should fight for one's home?'

'I...' Benjamin hesitates, his eyes straining for direction in the dark. 'When I left I was still too young to serve. I don't know what I would do if they called me up now.'

'You're safe here.'

'I know but...'

'Do you think that youth will be a valid excuse, when they come to do the final accounts? Because gender isn't, nor politics, nor ethnicity. We are branded by our names and our customs: we are not allowed to be neutral.'

He stops and leans against a piece of wall which must have once served a purpose but is now left useless at the side of the path, unconnected to any structure. Benjamin positions himself beside him and takes the proffered cigarette. After the initial burst of flame, there is just the inconstant rhythm of the two glowing tips moving back and forwards in the night.

'Will you go back?' Benjamin asks suddenly.

'I'm not a soldier.'

'Some people think you are a spy.'

An abrupt, hollow noise escapes Azad's throat and he realises that it was meant as a laugh.

'They've heard you speaking Lithuanian and Russian.'

'All educated people speak Russian.'

'Not like you do.'

'And what do you think, young Benjamin? Which side do you think I am spying for?'

Benjamin shifts his weight and flicks the cigarette butt out into the darkness.

'I know - you wouldn't be here if you thought that.' Azad's voice is low and calm and it stretches out into the silence with the tones of thankfulness.

'I was thinking of leaving,' after a long silence, the words burst out of Benjamin's mouth like food which cannot be kept down.

'What do you mean?'

'You know, getting out of Lithuania, trying to start up somewhere else.'

'What does your father say?'

'Last time he wrote, he told us all to go. He said that this war will go on for years, that there won't be a future fit for young people for a long time to come. And I was thinking about what you were saying, about them wanting to wipe us off the face of the earth. Maybe you're right. And if we stay here they will send us back as soon as there's a ceasefire and then it'll just be a question of time, before they start again.'

'And if you leave?'

'We can start again somewhere else. They won't have won, you see. We will go on living and growing.'

'Survival above all else.'

'Don't you think?'

Benjamin's voice is tentative, seeking confirmation, but he does not reply for some minutes.

'It's not so easy to get out.'

'There's Lucy. We've talked about the possibilities.'

His body is very still, as if any stray movement would reveal his feelings.

Benjamin goes on, unaware, 'We even talked about marrying, that way there would be no problem in getting a visa. At least for me at first and then we could apply later for my sister and mother.'

Impulsively, Azad pushes against the hard stone and stands up. He can feel the heat of the cigarette on his fingertips as it burns into the filter and throws it on the ground. 'If you think that's the right thing to do...'

There is a snap of sharp movement as Benjamin turns to him in the dark and he wonders if he hasn't managed to keep the spite out of his voice.

'You don't think it is right? I know she's not a Muslim but I was never brought up to be religious. Just to observe certain rules...of course...you know how it is. With us it is more a matter of tradition.'

'And her?'

Benjamin shrugs, as if the question is irrelevant, 'You know how they are in the West – it's not an issue. I've never known her go to church or anything. We've never even discussed it.'

He resists the desire to hurt, the vengeful inclination to let his doubts weed themselves into Benjamin's untainted mind.

'Don't ask me what is right; you have to go to the imam for that. If she agrees, then what have you got to lose?'

'You make it sound so harsh. It's not like that, I....I would take care of her.'

His mouth is dry, forcing him to swallow before he can answer. 'You have to do what you have to do.'

He has already started to move away and Benjamin follows, reluctantly. He can sense that there are more questions, more reassurances to be sought, but he no longer has the desire to talk. It is as if suddenly he can physically feel that hard, metallic object which lies beneath his mattress like a tumour beneath the skin and must go home to nurse it.

13

The sound of knocking is already registered somewhere in his half-consciousness and for a few seconds he starts to dream of the crack of grenades as they fall onto the wall of his house, the groaning of the tanks as they prepare to demolish. When the noise reaches his own room, he sits up with a start and in the rush of reality realises that it is simply the sound of a hand rapping on wood, moving from door to door down the long corridor.

'Boutique from eight-thirty till ten! First come, first served!' a male voice calls flatly.
Still sitting upright, he curses and pulls back the covers.
Pale turns towards him with half-open eyes, 'What's going on?'
'Clothes delivery - don't need anything?'
Pale groans; his eyes have already closed again and he rolls over, making the bed creak under his weight. 'The market is full of cheap Turkish stuff. I pick it up for almost nothing.'

Azad grunts and takes his clothes and wash-bag from the peg by the door, passing by Ismail's already vacated bed. There has been discussion in the camp as to whether there should be a call for prayer played over the loud speaker system five times a day but the issue is still unresolved: there is still some strength left in the fading voices of opposition.

There is a queue at the showers and he has to stand in line with four elderly men dressed in the white, sleeveless vests which were issued to each male at the beginning of the year. At the other end of the corridor he can see the much longer queue of women who have congregated outside the female cubicles. Their facilities are larger only in that they contain four deep sinks for washing clothes and drying racks, in addition to the three standard shower cubicles. He does not engage in conversation with the other men and each of them stands silently, their eyes fixed on internal images. Every time the sound of water stops there is a pause before the lock is flipped back and the door is opened, precipitating a forward shuffle from those waiting.

He showers quickly, conscious of the men still waiting outside and pulls on his jeans and shirt over his damp body. The 'boutique' is the refugee's tongue-in-cheek name for the tiny room where the Red Cross hand out donated clothes once a month. The clothes are brought in by van in the early morning, smelling of the chemical sanitizer with which they are sprayed once they are sorted. Some of the donations, the smaller part, come from local people who leave the plastic bags full of unwanted and out-grown garments he sometimes sees deposited outside the head office in the middle of town. But the majority comes from abroad; from the excess collected in warehouses across Europe and shipped by truck to areas of need. The popular items, the good quality trousers and jumpers, go quickly and often when he arrives there are only cheap acrylic shirts and worn-out suits left limp on the metal hangers. Today he will try to take his quota: after the incident with Thomas, he can no longer rely on his cousin's generosity - the odd T-shirt, a pair of jeans bought from the market, gifts for New Year or birthday.

Out on the tarmac, there is already a group of people waiting beside the administration block: a loose knot of humanity jostling with the imperative of their own needs. Azad positions himself beside them, near enough to indicate his presence in the queue yet not close enough to be drawn into their discussion. The sun is very low in the sky today and there are dark, heavy clouds which seem to hang just above their heads. On days like these, it seems as if there is no colour left in the world – and for him this is worse than the layer of snow which will come later, for that brings a kind of peace in its absence of tone. Creeping in on them from the cooling woods and the stormy sea, he can sense the cold approaching like an oppressor from the East. These early winter days, when the leaves have already fallen and the trees stand like burnt corpses, fill him with a sense of abandonment which is hard to shake off.

As the crowd moves slowly closer to its destination, the space around him diminishes, until he finds himself in the centre of a tight ball of bodies. He can recognise the smell of sweat, the odour of mustiness which comes off the sheets and blankets, the lingering stink of garlic and dried meats. Yet in the midst of all this, the remembrance of Zahra's own scent comes to him with a sudden smile: like soft, white bread when you pull it apart in your hands. In spite of the on-coming winter and the bleakness of the camp, he indulges himself in images of her, of the comfort of having someone to wake up to. There is an essential part of him which sees a natural sense of order in the two of them being together, for there have always been females in his life; taking care of him, listening to his problems, absorbing the burden of being himself in the padded softness of their flesh.

'Keep moving or you'll lose your place!'
He turns to see Benjamin's mother positioning herself into the slot behind him, her large breasts unavoidable beneath the tight material of her blouse and cardigan. She is a phlegmatic character, accepting of every passing change in the political climate with the same jaded forbearance. For her the future of their country and its people lie not in the strength of armies or the manoeuvres of politicians but in the blighted destiny of a people caught on a geographic and ethnic fault line. It is the

philosophy of the elderly which he remembers from his youth, from the coffee bars and trader's stalls of his quarter.

'Don't worry, I'm marking my territory,' he replies.

'Eh,' she cocks her head and makes a clicking noise with her tongue, 'heaven knows we have to fight for every crumb in this place.'

Over her hair, she wears a headscarf: not one of those thick, charity-less ones worn by the religious women but a floral one which is bound loosely beneath her chin like the peasant women in the market. Curls of spirally black hair poke out from under it like shoots sprouting up from the cracks in the pavement.

'Did you see the news yesterday?' she asks, almost furtively.

'Of course.' His voice is low, so as to avoid the inclusion of the others who surround them.

She shakes her head rhythmically from side to side, as if in an act of mourning, 'God save their souls.'

Sensing the subject matter of their conversation, the crowd around them start to stir like animals woken rudely from their sleep. The sound is indefinable: the murmur of disapproval, sounds of agreement and dissent.

'There will be nothing left to save, after they have finished! If they hadn't rebelled against the government in the first place, there would have been no killing.' An elderly man, his lips curled around the butt of a cigarette, shouts in their direction.

For a moment, there is a silence of shocked realisation, as if the judgement of a condemned man had been uttered. There seems to be only the faintest breeze of resistance moving in-between them.

'There was killing enough before! They were just waiting for an excuse!'

'Those people were lost before they began!'

Voices call out randomly, their identities lost in the crowd.

'You can't talk like that – it's only for God to decide who is doomed. It is always people's right to hope.'

It is Benjamin's mother who finally stills the arguments, her body brought up to its full height as if in defiance of anyone that would try to question her right.

'Inshalla,' someone mutters from the crowd; the words closing the gap of fear which had been opening up in the face of despair. It is as if they have all been reprieved from their sentences: given permission to believe again.

'Next!'

The voice from inside the building, with the distinctive Lithuanian slant distorting the Russian words, seems to come from another reality. The crowd falter, as if thrown by the sudden realisation of their situation and the woman nearest enters the building while the rest wait in silence.

***

Once he has taken his allotted number of items from the Red Cross store he makes he way back to the barrack to arrange for them to be laundered. In the wake of the incident at Alma's house, he has been forced to make an agreement with one of the old women on his corridor. She will wash and iron for him, and in return he will carry out any minor repairs in her room. As there are only a handful of men in the centre without wives or sisters to wash for them, it is taken for granted that other women will take on the obligation for small favours in return. It is Pale who has made the best deal; calling on a middle-aged widow once a week in the middle of the night and having a neat pile of clean clothes gratefully waiting for him every Friday.

By the time he has deposited his clothes in his room, he is already anxious to escape the camp for the city. Today is a study day for him, yet he prefers the anonymity of the central library as a place to close himself away and concentrate. Returning to his room briefly to collect his coat, he passes the still-sleeping figure of Pale and closes the door quietly. His feet hurry him across the forecourt and out the gate, passing by his bicycle, still safely chained inside the border fence yet rendered useless by the frost and wind of a fast-approaching Lithuanian winter.

The streets of the city are busy with lunchtime traffic and the bus crawls along Pylimo Avenue, jolting with each pothole and the avoidance of every un-signalled manoeuvre. He is almost thrown out onto the pavement by the sudden stop and the premature opening of the doors and is immediately caught up in the friction of movement, the impetus of purpose which characterises normal life. Only here can he find some kind of relief from the unhealthy inertia of the camp, the endless routine waiting: for meals, for deliveries of clothes and hygienic supplies, for the evening transmission of the news in their native tongue on the pirate radio stations, for the end of the war. As he likes to tell any new person that he meets; he is an expert in waiting among a people who have perfected the art.

Heading northwards, he turns left at the junction into Pamenkalno, walking along the near side of pavement instead of crossing immediately in order to head down towards the river. It is not a street he has ever visited before and impulsively he stops outside an incongruous wooden house which is painted green and set back from the roadside in a well-kept garden. There is something about the smallness of it, the vulnerability of its thin planks amongst the stone and concrete, which makes him draw nearer, his eye immediately catching the symbol of a seven-stick candelabra which rests above the door. Seeing a man appear at the doorway, he hesitates and half turns his head away, yet continues to watch furtively as the dark figure emerges; his body clad in a long back robe, two perfectly formed ringlets falling from either side of his wide black hat.

When the man has safely moved away down the street the house seems once again deserted. He moves closer in order to inspect the small sign to the left of the main door, making out the words 'Jewish State Museum'. Despite his curiosity there is an uncomfortable feeling that he is trespassing here, and he waits on the pavement, caught again in the inertia of indecision. Then very slowly, he steps up to the door and tries the handle, which gives way easily to his touch and opens onto a hallway where a solitary woman sits at a desk in the far corner, framed by bookcases. She smiles briefly and then lowers her head towards the book which lays open in her lap.

Now that he is inside, it doesn't seem that he is breaking any laws of conduct: the rooms which stretch out from the hallway, with their polished parquet floors and neat glass display boxes seem safe - diffused of any sense of condemnation. Moving past the desk, he wanders from one display case to another, unable to identify the significance of the objects laid out for inspection- the scrolls of parchment on heavy golden rods, the leather bound books and strips of embroidered material – the paraphernalia of a religion which he has only read about and which seems as remote from him as the golden domes of the Orthodox Cathedrals or the processions of saints which he has seen pass through the streets of the old town. It is as if he has stepped out of the known world into a place where he can only ever be a stranger; a world of history and beliefs which can never be comprehended without the painstaking layering of daily practice.

But in the second room the content of the display starts to change into something more menacing and immediately more recognisable; rusted handcuffs and chains, small yellow stars sewn onto armbands. There are lists of laws and regulations stamped with the Eagle of the Third Reich, translated into Lithuanian and English on yellowing cards typed out on a typewriter. He examines each object one by one, alone amongst the relics of dead people, hearing only the rhythm of his breath as he moves softly around the hushed room. Surrounded by the detritus of massacre, the room is nothing more than a cemetery for him, filled with the ghosts of the extinct and the unknown. On the far wall there hangs a list of names which resound with an exotic unfamiliarity in his mind as he repeats them to himself methodically: Hiam, Shlomo, Efriam, all with the same year of death: 1943.

It is in only the final room, displaying enlarged copies of old black and white photographs of Vilnius, that he experiences an odd sensation of something familiar, of reality dislocated. The array of grainy images show a town at once recognizable and yet foreign and remote: the narrow, cobbled alleyways and high walls of the Vilnius ghetto, the idiosyncratic criss-cross of paths and streets interrupted by the dark shadows of doorways and corridors which lead off the page into scenes of a now obsolete way of life. The figures which line the borders of these pictures, in their colourless coats and hats, are smudged and undefined, as if already ghosts. He cannot make out individual features; there is just the tilt of a head, the black gash of a mouth shouting, a huddled mass of bodies herded into a corner. With painstaking detail, the plans for the imprisonment of an entire people within the walls of their own homes are outlined on maps which are thrown up mercilessly onto the high, white walls.

There is no noise except the hum of the projectors mounted on the ceilings. He stands, his head thrown back awkwardly so as to trace the lines of enclosure, as if comprehension of this strange geography will give him the key to understanding the machinations of hatred. He can no longer feel the border of himself: the flesh and hair which define the end of his own body and the start of the objects around him seem to have melted into one another.

It is only with the small, unexpected human noise of someone coughing that he is shifted back to reality. In confusion, he turns and sees the unusually short figure of the woman from the reception standing at a discreet distance.
'We close at twelve today,' she tells him in English, having already classified him as not of this place.
He nods and lets his eyes search her face, but she twitches uncomfortably and quickly turns away. He is wondering if she belongs to this race whose attempted destruction he has tried to decipher amongst discarded belongings and yellowed images. As he moves back towards the foyer, he walks by a room he had not yet reached, over which there hangs a sign 'Hall of the Righteous.' The woman does not look up again as he passes her, but as he lets the door close behind him he can hear the gentle click of the lock turning. From the outside, the building seems deserted; as if a house which is lived-in gives out a different sense of itself than one which is only worked in. Walking down the five wooden steps which lead back onto the pavement, he suddenly recalls being a child and leaving his mother in hospital to recover from the lung infection which nearly killed her.

'What are you up to?'
A familiar voice startles him, and he reels around abruptly, as if he has been caught doing something illicit.
'I didn't know this was your part of town?'
The voice belongs to Blacky: tight jeans and black leather jacket zipped up over a green woollen scarf.
'I was on my way to town.... just meandering,' he is irked by his own feeling of guilt and speaks gruffly.

Blacky smirks as if amused by his discomfort, then leans in closer as if to impart a secret. 'It's all Heebs around here, you should be careful – not being kosher.'

Blacky makes this last comment in Lithuanian, mimicking the Vilnius accent with surprising accuracy.

'You hang around too much with the wrong kind of locals.'

'It's the only way to make a living.'

'Would you know a Jew if you fucked one?'

Blacky laughs then looks up at the building behind them; an undefined inkling of discomfort welling up inside him.

'I hear you're going to get married, Azad. Were the bonds of love sealed in my room?'

'What do you know about it?'

'Nothing!' Blackie throws out his arms in a gesture of innocence and his eyes once again move to the small green building and the tell-tale sign, 'just wanted to give my congratulations.'

Impulsively, he shifts his weight into a walk, forcing Blacky to move with him. Crossing the street towards a tall glass office building, they are already a world away from the frail house and the bleak array of artefacts.

'Have you been contacted?'

They are standing quite close together, and yet Azad is not sure he has heard the words correctly. Confused, it takes him a few seconds to realise their significance, yet remarkably he manages to keep his face immobile despite the fluttering of his insides.

'What are you talking about?'

There is only a split second of hesitation, a brief moment of surprise, before Blacky continues,

'By the imam… I understood the imam is to arrange the marriage. I met Benjamin yesterday and he told me it would be a traditional ceremony.'

The delivery is smooth, no wrinkles in the cloth, so that he is left wondering if he only imagined the reference. Just a few hours before, his fingers had checked for the small bulge at the edge of the mattress.

'I expect him any day.'

'Fine, fine. It's a good thing to have a woman by you, to start a family, to start to plan for the future.'

There is an emphasis on the word 'plan', a tiny push for recognition which is over as soon as it is said.

'And what are your plans?'

'Ah,' Blacky flicks his head aside, as if avoiding a blow, 'I don't have any plans for the moment. My mother's employers give me work from time to time. I'm surviving quite well for now.'

He lets out a grunt by way of reply and pats Blacky on the back, letting the weight of his arm rest for a few moments before turning to leave.

'*La Ilaha Ila Allah* - there is no God but Allah'

Blacky's words reach him only after he has started walking away.

14

For the past few days he has done nothing but study and sleep, staying at the faculty until the library closes at nine, then taking the bus back to the refugee centre when most of its inhabitants are already closed inside their rooms. In that way, he has managed to avoid meeting Benjamin or even Pale, who goes to bed religiously at ten every evening in order to be able to get up for his five a.m. shifts. For him the maintenance of this rhythm is like escape to a place where life carries him along without the need for active thought or decision. Like this, he can lose himself in routine of white walls and artificial lights; the thin covering of morning frost on the grass and bushes which border the roadside; the dullness of the industrial buildings seen from the misted windows of the bus.

Today, as usual, he got up at six and arrived just as the doors to the university building were being opened by the sleepy night watchman. Now that his lectures are over, he makes his way through the crowded midday corridors towards the lunch hall. Being a student without private means, he is allotted twenty food tickets each month which entitle him to the daily cooked meal and a hot drink. Only on the days when pork is on offer does he have to use his own money to buy food.

Entering the canteen, he throws his bag carelessly onto a bench and joins the queue of students waiting to order: he can already smell the odours of fried meat and cabbage mixed in with the scent of coffee from the bar. The place is busy and noisy as always, and at first he does not notice the images flickering across the screen of the TV mounted above the tills on the far wall. It is only as he moves closer to the counter that something familiar catches his eye and he stops dead still in order to look closer at the frighteningly familiar scene. The sound is turned down so low that he cannot hear what the presenter is saying, yet the pictures can be deciphered by every nerve in his body.

The footage must have been taken with a video camera, for its images are grainy and it is hard to work out the individual features of the faces which the camera scans with unconcealed pride, recording every detail of defeat. His countrymen are being led out of the blackened door of a breeze block shelter (where are the women?). Emaciated, too traumatised to be frightened, they pay no attention to the camera that captures their humiliation. The film stops abruptly and the screen is full of over-used shots of mountain scenes – the cragged cliffs and valleys of the region where he grew up; the camera sweeping and ducking and the shadow of a helicopter thrown onto the pale, flattened grass far below. The scene cuts again to the studio and the face of the presenter, stern and unyielding, mouthing details which his own mind races to reconstruct.

Not able to stand the silence any longer, he uses a chair to climb onto a table, bringing him up just below the television. Already people nearby have turned around to see what is going on; watching curiously as he prizes open the control panel and twists the dial to full. Abruptly, a shrill voice distorted by volume fills the open space around them:

"...by 6.45 the government forces had already broken through the main line of defence, along the ridge of the ....slopes. This film, taken by a paramilitary soldier at the scene of the final surrender and downloaded onto a Russian news website at 12 noon, confirms the confused reports that had been filtering out all morning. The recapture of the valley marks a drastic change

in the balance of the conflict, with the government claiming victory and the defeat of terrorist enclaves in the towns of ....."

He feels his body jerk at the name of his hometown twisted awkwardly by the foreign pronunciation, yet still capable of squeezing the breath out of his chest. It seems as if everyone in the hall has been forced to attention by the intrusion of the voice, before a brisk movement to his right plunges them all into silence. In the last few seconds of speech he had been aware of a voice shouting to him from his side but it is only now, with the sound of TV cut, that he registers his professor's up-turned face staring at him with a mixture of defiance and uncertainty. The sudden cutting of the power supply has left a brief hiatus which still vibrates with the words of the commentator – the air hanging momentarily in neutrality before crashing down in the confusion of discussion. Simultaneously, he jumps down from the table and strides out, without a glance at the still stationary figure or the faces following him with eyes half afraid to look.

He doesn't bother to take his bag from the table where he left it. Too intent on trying to understand where he should go and what he should do, his mind and body are no longer connected to that time- just two minutes and one lifetime ago- when he was pretending so well to be an ordinary student in the third year of his studies. His feet lead him down the corridor and across the foyer, where it seems his shoes clatter unbearably loudly on the marble tiled floor. Outside, the frosty air slaps his face as he swings open the heavy glass doors, and immediately the remembrance of suffering flashes through his mind: his people have been hungry and cold for a long time: since the frosts arrived in early October they have been subject to the slow torture of starvation and despair – the ever increasing volume of the grenade attacks, the ricocheting of bullets and the crackle of fire. They say that the smell of human flesh is putrid.

He does not know how he will be able to find out if the names of his mother and the rest of his family are on the list of survivors (is there a list?). His mind reels with the absurd protocol of war (there must be a list- but made by whom? - the Red Cross, the Red Crescent…he must go to their offices and register the names of those he wants to find).

The car must have been crawling next to him for a while, for when he looks down into the face of Alma he can see an incredulous fear contorting her familiar features. It seems to him that it takes a long time to link her face to the moment and to untwine it from those of the dead and missing which fill his vision but perhaps his impulse to get into the seat beside her is stronger than his imagination; for only a few seconds elapse before he is sitting next to her.

She waits for him to get in and shut the door before she checks her mirror and pulls out. He doesn't speak or even look at her.
'I searched for you at the centre.' She pauses for a moment, acknowledging the mutual awareness that this is the first time she has seen the place he lives. 'Your room mate told me you would probably be here.'
He nods, unable to find the words that would be the normal answer to such a statement.
'I called the house…' her voice trails off, as if it is only now that she is aware of the ridiculousness of the act.
'The government issued a statement stating that they have no statistics on survivors at present but that they are coordinating with the Red Cross to get civilians out as soon as possible.'
'The government!' he spits the phrase out of his mouth with a vengeance which starkly contrasts her calm rationality.
'It's all we've got.'

He retreats into silence again, watching the icy pavement slide smoothly under the car, letting himself be driven without an idea of where it is they have to go.

Alma too shrinks away from the things which neither of them dares to say: it is the traffic lights and the changing of the gears and the tiny, everyday habits which must save them from the horror of the unimaginable.

'The Red Cross need to have a list of the names…for identification.'

'We can do it in the morning,' she snaps, then adds more gently, 'or I will call them later, from home. We don't have to go there to queue with all those other…..'

They are reaching the edge of the city now, to the estates of socialist apartment blocks and municipal playgrounds and the unavoidable melancholia of a failed dream. They pass by the bus terminal, where the rusty hulks of broken vehicles are lined up as if to protect each other from obsolescence.

At the junction his eyes flit towards the turning for the refugee centre but Alma steers out onto the motorway without comment. In his twelve months here he has only been out of the city once, on a coach trip to the coast organised by a Swedish charity.

'Where do you think you're going?'

'To the countryside… I thought we could walk, get away from the city and the TV and…. I don't know. I want to take you away from there.'

'Take me back.'

His voice is unusually low and there is something about its insistence which scares her. She takes her eyes briefly away from the road in order to look at him properly but he avoids her gaze: she knows him too well.

'I don't ….' she begins.

'I need to go back.'

She does not slow down and an exit passes them by, its green signs pointing uselessly into the air. He sighs and puts his hand on hers where it rests on the gear stick; his fingers exerting the smallest amount of pressure.

'We can't do this. We can't pretend it didn't happen.'

She glances again at him, then lets out a cry. Instinctively, he leans over and manages to steer the car into the emergency lane, for her hands have started to tremble so much that she no longer has control of the vehicle.

When they are at a halt, he gets out the car and comes around to open her door. Almost lifting her, he helps her into the passenger seat, feeling even through the woollen coat the jerking of her limbs from the sobs which rupture inside her. Then he gets in the driver's seat and starts the car; his eyes dry as bone as they concentrate on the lines of traffic speeding past them. Alma has curled herself into a small ball beside him on the seat, as if trying to protect herself against the blows of an assailant.

They do not speak on the drive back home and by the time he pulls in at the lay-by opposite her apartment block, she has lulled herself into a moaning calm. The stopping of the engine and the pulling of the brakes make her raise her head and she seems surprised to find the familiar surroundings still intact.

'Is Thomas in?'

His tone is calm and firm, forcing her back to the reality around her. She shakes her head and reaches in her bag for the keys, which she passes to him. She is ten years older than him but it is he who must take control.

Inside the house the television is still on, its low tones vibrating through the empty rooms. Wordlessly, he goes into the kitchen to make coffee while Alma makes her way to the bathroom. He can hear the door lock behind her and it is only then that his throat lets out the involuntary sob from inside him. It is over in a second and happens only once.

He takes the coffee pot from the shelf and unscrews the bottom part, then goes to the tap and fills it to the brim. The stove is electric and he flicks the switch to heat up the ring before spooning in the brown powder from the tin on the shelf. His movements are slow and precise and he follows each step carefully in order to keep anything else from entering his consciousness. He knows from experience that this is the only way to keep going; to cling to the little tasks like a drowning man to a life raft.

When he has put everything on a tray – the coffee pot, the cups standing upright on their saucers, two tall glasses of tap water, the sugar glistening in the bowl – he comes into the living room and seats himself on the sofa next to Alma. Her face is dry now, her make-up re-touched around the eyes and a smudge of rouge worked into the pale cheeks.
'Thomas hasn't even called. He must have heard what happened.'
He does not answer, noticing the still light of the answer phone at her side.
She takes the bottle of pills that is resting in her lap and tipping three into her hand, washes them down with a glass of water. Then she throws him the bottle but he puts it back carefully onto the table, before reaching forward to pour the coffee.

***

It seems like a very long time before he finally feels that it is safe to leave Alma. Only after the cycle of panic and recriminations have wound themselves down to a tight coil of resignation and he can once again trust her instinct for self-preservation and the dulling effects of the tablets, does he get up from beside her near-sleeping body on the couch and slip noiselessly out the front door.

Outside, away from the imperative of care, he feels a chill which penetrates his bones more than the wind and the frost: a biting sense of loneliness which seems to have come from the very centre of his being and causes him to gasp in surprise. He stops and looks down at the pavement, the pitted grey surface pocked with the uneven marks of old stains and the smooth circles of chewing gum now become part of the asphalt. Bending down, he lets his hand run along the cold, rough surface, as if reassuring himself of its solidity.

When he stands up again, he is filled with the urgent need to be in the physical presence of another human being, to unburden himself of the weight of survival. His feet carry him forward in what is almost a run and he moves back in the direction of the only home he possesses. He is not conscious of the landscape around him but only of this sensation of need, of a hunger to belong, to possess and be possessed, as if he can no longer stand the hardship of being alone with himself.

When he finally reaches the centre, he does not go to his room but turns instead into the first barrack and straight down the corridor towards her room. Without thinking, he raps loudly on the door, stepping forward so that he will be right up close against whoever opens it. When the figure of the her father appears in the narrow doorway, he thrusts himself even closer, 'I need to see Zahra.'
The old man flinches at the proximity of the body which blocks him and is forced to look closely at his face: at the dark shadows which hang beneath his eyes like bruises, the jaw sharp with tension.

'We did not agree to this.'

'Have you not heard the news?'

His voice is full of the same frustrated incomprehension he felt at their first meeting; the horrible realisation of the impossibility of mutual understanding. The old man hesitates, drawing his lower lip under his teeth and making a low, sucking sound.

'Have I not agreed to everything you asked? Can't you leave us ten minutes of peace?'

There is a pause in which neither of them speaks.

'Or is there no charity in the hard place of your belief?'

There is a movement from inside the room and a murmur which draws the old man back inside, his right hand still clutching the door as if unwilling to relinquish his dominion. When he turns back, he nods for Azad to enter, keeping his eyes averted.

Inside the curtains are drawn; their thin, orange tone obscuring the stuffy interior. In the middle of the room Zahra has been made to sit on the ugly, metal chair which he used on his last visit; so much more neutral than the suggested intimacy of the beds. The mother does not acknowledge his presence but walks over to the window and with one swift flick of her wrist, lets in the light. Columns of dust swirl violently in the sudden movement of air.

'We will wait outside,' she states.

The elderly couple shuffle slowly out of the room and let the door close gently behind them, so that it falls just short of shutting. He smiles at their distrust and turns to the expectant figure in front of him. Zahra's eyes do not meet his, her head averted to the side as if to avoid a blow and he is temporarily at a loss for how to react. Then he sits down on the bed to her left.

'Did you hear what happened?'

She lifts her face towards him, the softness of her features hardened by the dark blue of the cloth which is wrapped tightly around her head and fastened in front with two pins.

'We have been watching the Russian channels all morning. They said that they are negotiating for prisoners, there's still a chance...'

He smiles without humour and looks at her without speaking for so long that she blushes.

'We should get away from here.'

'What do you mean?'

'From here: this fucking centre, this country.'

'I don't understand. We are supposed...next week.'

'Next week?' Uncomprehending, he looks at her as if he does not know what she is referring to; as if he no longer believes in next week or the contract which they have agreed to.

'My parents were going to send word to you today.'

Shy in the face of his confusion, she does not dare to mention the word, 'the imam told us he will discuss the final arrangements with you.'

'What difference does that make now? Don't you understand what has happened? What this means? There will be no home to go back to anymore, no job, no life there as we once knew it.'

'You don't know that. You don't know what will happen. We can't just forget everything and run. You have your mother there.'

'Do you think there will be anyone left when they are finished?'

She starts, and her hand twitches as if it would reach for him if only she dared.

'We have to wait and hope.'

Her voice is quiet but firm in its insistence; it is the old adage he has heard from the mouths of every woman in the camp.

'We have to hope,' he mimics, 'always bloody hope. Don't you realise that it is hope that destroys us, tricks us into believing, into submission? Without hope we would be so much braver, so much more honest. Hope is a loser's game.'

Her eyes have become wider now and he can tell that she is afraid. He would shout, would grab her by the shoulders and make her understand but he is intensely aware of the figures behind the glass following every sound, monitoring every movement.

'Don't you understand? We are the losers, ordinary people are the losers. We have already lost this war, if we don't go now there will be no more chances.'

'There are always ways to get out. We can choose to go anytime, when we are surer of what will happen.'

'I'm not talking about visas. There will be no more chances for us to save ourselves, don't you understand?'

He lets out a sigh and raises his hand to his left eye, then rubs his fingers lightly over the closed lid.

'Look at you. Look at this place and what it has made of us.'

Zahra's features seem to tighten, as if she is suddenly reminded of the drab cloth which encloses them.

'It seems ridiculous…I didn't imagine it would be like this but maybe I should have known. Everything has changed since coming here. My parents were not the people you see now.'

'I didn't come to talk about that. It's over now.'

'I hate that you were forced…'

'*We* were forced: forced to leave our homes, forced to live like cattle. If we are made to marry, is it such a bad thing? For two people to look after each other…'

He reaches out and grasps her hands where they lay in her lap and lets his fingers run gently up her forearm so that the skin ripples in response.

'But that doesn't mean that they can force us into a life we do not want. If we want to be together, it doesn't have to be their decision…'

Her body has slackened under his touch but her mind is still full of the feminine wariness which she has been bred on.

'You cannot live your life for them,' he continues, 'if we have the possibility to follow a different path, the strength to get up and leave, we have to take that chance.'

'I can't think like you. There's no mercy in what you are saying. I feel like you've condemned them all, that you think we are the only ones worth saving.'

'Aren't we?'

'But they are our people: this is who we are. Why do you try to deny that?'

All at once he has the sensation that it is not Zahra who stares at him but the face of an unknown woman from a newspaper photograph or a TV report; he can no longer recognise the particular features of someone he knows, someone whose breath he has felt on his shoulder as he sleeps. The feeling lasts no longer than a second but when it has passed, there is an absence in its wake.

He is saved from the finality of words by the opening of the door and the return of Zahra's parents. They make no apology for their unannounced arrival and he gets up automatically, passing them by with a brief nod of his head. Perhaps they expect a gesture of thanks or acknowledgement, for they look at him with offended suspicion; or perhaps it is only the tangible presence of desolation on his body which shocks them.

15

'There's post for you in the office.'

'Couldn't you bring it?'

Pale shrugs his shoulders, 'it's a packet – they want you to sign for it.'

He looks at him uncomprehendingly but Pale has already turned and is putting on his hat and coat. When the door is shut behind him, he gets up from the bed and pulls on a sweater. He has not eaten anything all day and for a moment he feels a light-headedness which makes him reach for the bedside table in order to steady himself.

Outside, the place is deserted. There are not even the usual groups of children playing ball on the worn pitch or sitting on the benches to exchange football cards. He walks briskly to the office building, the cold penetrating his thin clothes like water. The woman on duty looks at him without expression, then points to a pile of white and beige envelopes which are stacked to her side. He picks up a wad and starts to sort through them, finding the one addressed to him almost immediately.

'Sign here,' her thin index finger directs him to a log book open on the desk in front of her, and he scribbles his signature next to the entry with his name and the date.

The packet is a folded piece of cardboard with the address printed and stuck onto the front. He can see that the postmark is local. Pulling back the adhesive seal, he breaks open the card to find an unmarked disc in a plastic folder and realises with a cold chill that this is the accompaniment to the previous gift that still lies hidden beneath his mattress. Hastily, he wraps it again in its cardboard covering and runs across the courtyard back to his room. Once inside, he pushes a chair against the wall and quickly pulls himself through the window, pushing it closed behind him. Exiting via the broken fence, he makes his way across the scrubland until he meets up with the road five hundred metres from the barracks, where he turns and walks westwards. The streets are almost empty – a lunchtime lull before the start of the traffic jams which mark the end of school and the seven till three shift, and it doesn't take him long to arrive at the place he wants to go.

Entering the deserted space, he catches the eye of the barmaid and gestures towards the computer which is set up in the far corner of the room. There is a panelled partition near the terminal and this he pulls around him as far as it will go, before sitting down and inserting the disc. The computer is old and over-used, so that at first there is nothing but a blank screen and a noise like an engine starting up. He can feel the heat of the hard disc working next to the cold denim of his trousers.

He does not dare to imagine what it is that he is waiting for – the guttural insistence of Arabic and the rhythmic sound of prayers or the desperate eyes of his compatriots pleading for a return to the values which he has never known? But when the images appear on the screen, he is struck by the unexpected familiarity of it. The film is of low quality; rendering the colours artificially bright and the faces unrefined, yet immediately he can recognise his hometown – the street corners and buildings which he has traced in his mind so many times since he left that they have taken on the stuff of fairy tales. With incomprehension, he moves his head closer to the screen so that he is as near as he can be without the images disintegrating into meaningless grains.

The camera scans the streets: the grey blocks of flats with the ubiquitous graffiti, the tarmac worn down by years of bad maintenance and shelling, the facades pocked with the scattered marks of shrapnel like a disease that spreads up from street level and threatens to infest the whole construction. His town looks like an old man who has been beaten by the elements for so long that he isn't even aware of his own state of dilapidation. Only now and then can he spot a house still intact or a green square of parkland which recalls the ordered, peaceful place where he grew up.

Following a slow and steady course, the film weaves past the main square, with its vacant podium where once a statue of Lenin stood proud, and along the Boulevard of the Victims of Fascism (no doubt they have changed the name of this now too?). The pictures bump and sway with the rhythm of the cameraman walking; heightening the impression of being part of the virtual reality. He knows the route well, for it is the same way he took every morning to his school. He can even recall the smell of the bakery that would never fail to lure him inside with the warm aroma of bread and cakes, and the stench of ammonia from the factory which would waft across from the east of the city on a windy day.

Abruptly, the camera turns right, leading him between high, narrow buildings and out onto a parallel road. There are still trees standing here, their leaves casting a molten shadow on the grey of the pavement and walls, so that he realises that these images are from the summer which has just passed, making them more recent that any of the ones his memory owns. For a few seconds the pictures disappear behind a curtain of static and then there is only blackness. He stares intently, as if willing them to restart, and all of a sudden the colours return and jolt themselves into a recognisable form. But this is a very different view: instead of the sunlight and open air, he is thrust under the harsh strip lights of a bleak interior. At first, his mind cannot register where the camera has taken him, for there are no reference points to cling to; only a long white corridor and a tall window half covered in plastic. And then the angle changes and a row of narrow beds comes into view, and all at once he knows they are in the hospital.

It is just like the footage he has seen on news broadcasts – the tense faces of family members poised above the prone bodies of their loved ones while the nurses and doctors work around them with doomed efficiency. And yet this time there is a difference: the camera zooms in on the bruised and terrified face of a young woman, then moves slowly down her body as closely as a lover would. The neck is exposed and the white gown falls loosely over her breasts, but below her waist where her legs should be there is only a tangled mess of bloodied rags and a horrible lack of solidity.

Suddenly, the camera jerks into motion beside the bed, leading him down a hallway and into a large room which he can instantly recognise as the operating theatre. The sound, until now a background noise of mumbling and footsteps, opens out into a piercing scream of fear. As if responding to this audio cue, there is a scramble of arms and bodies, a moment of wrestling which ends in the image of the woman held down by a number of nurses and men wearing civilian clothes. He can see a bottle of vodka resting on one of the benches along with an array of sharp metal saws and grotesque instruments.

There is a hiatus - a desperate rush of disbelief before the inevitable tragedy of necessity. He has heard rumours of hospitals left without enough drugs and anaesthetics to treat the wounded but he has never allowed his mind to wander further down the corridors of consequence. The war has brought with it so many new horrors, and yet he finds himself so painfully unprepared for this one. And as if from a loud speaker, the voice of a man starts to spit out words of desperation and vengeance:

'Look what is happening to our people as a direct result of the government's embargo and aggression, the same government which the Western powers support and which keeps our women and children in poverty and suffering. If you have any pity in your heart, you cannot look on such scenes without the urge for justice welling up inside you. Only when this evil regime has been overthrown will there ever be peace in these lands - lands which should be united under Islam, the religion which we all share with our blood and our minds. Reek revenge on those whose imperialistic policies have kept our people trodden in the mud for hundreds of years...'

Instinctively, he leans forward and pauses the film; so that the voice is silenced and the screen is filled with the terrible gaze of a woman about to watch her own dissection. Her features jerk back and forth between motion and stillness as she is caught in timeless suspension and he stares at the distorted face, knowing that he does not have the strength to carry on watching.

'Are you going to drink something?'
He turns and fixes his eyes on the source of the voice, his words lost in an aching fracture of disbelief which for a few seconds cannot differentiate between the two realities. The barmaid shifts uncomfortably on her high heels, and her eyes flick instinctively behind him to the shifting image. Brought back to actuality by her look of surprise, he quickly leans forward and turns off the monitor, feeling her body move away as he does so. Slipping the thin disc of metal back into its cover he gets up to leave, hastily dropping a few banknotes onto the bar as he passes.

***

This is the half world between anger and desperation, an un-real time of waiting for the inevitable. Since the phone lines are all down, the only news from his homeland comes in the form of amateur videos shown on brief news broadcasts or the furious denouncements relayed from radio stations within Russia that can never be found twice on the same wavelength. He plays the game of living now like an amnesiac going through the motions of every routine without engagement, while his conscious mind crouches like a cat above its prey: vigilant, immobile, waiting for some small sign which will lead it back to the reality it once knew.

Lying on his bed in the twilight of evening, he tries to count how many hours have elapsed since he heard the news. Logically, he knows that it is only one day and one night which have passed, yet his recollection of yesterday morning is like a childhood memory, very small and vague beneath the weight of what has come between. There are no noises in the corridor now, no sound of people outside in the courtyard. Only occasionally will he hear a shuffle of shoes or the brief running of water, before the closing of a door. He looks at his watch: there are fifteen minutes to go before the official opening of the office where the Red Cross will take details of the missing persons. They have already been given the necessary forms along with breakfast rations; tiny squares of paper with instructions written in Russian and English. He has completed seven: one for his mother, for his uncle and aunt and for his four cousins. Seven, he remembers, is supposed to be a lucky number.

His breath is slow and the movement of his lungs is very shallow. The TV set in the corner of the room has been running all night, its sound turned down so low that it can hardly be heard against the other small noises of life going on around him. Despite his concentration on the thick glass of the screen, he is aware of every inch of skin on his body as it rubs up against the reality that surrounds it. It is as if he is no longer part of the space in which he fits, like a man whose house has suddenly filled with water and who finds that he has to exist in a shadowy, sub-marine world.

He watches the second hand move slowly around the dial of his watch and lets the minutes tick past twelve and into the second half of the day. He knows very well that he should get up and join the queue of people waiting in front of the low, breezeblock building. It is an exceptional visit, on behalf of the Red Cross, organised in order to avoid the mass movement of refugees to the downtown office. Here, along the un-asphalted road, behind the trees and the wire mesh fence, the protocol of salvage will be carried out.

When he finally pulls his weight up from the thin mattress, he finds his limbs stiff and unresponsive as if his body has been through a long sickness. Realising that his shoes are already tied onto his feet, he picks up the seven thin sheets of paper and shuffles out into the deserted corridor. Outside, there is only one focus of attention, around which every inhabitant is clustered.

The faces of the women that surround him are no longer the faces which he has come to know; they have been smoothed into expressionless masks with the whitewash of industrial drugs. There is no longer any possibility to look into a person's eyes and see there the scenes of a life once lived together, there is simply the plunge into the dreadful vacancy of either acknowledgement or denial. Just as in birth so in death, it is the women who carry the grief around with them like strangled babies abandoned in their wombs. The few men that are left seem resigned to be nothing but helpless observers – heads hung down, eyes staring only at the ground – standing noiselessly as if subdued by the force of female anguish.

The silence is rent by a faint hum which slowly builds up into a rumble. The noise descends from the distance and appears as two low white vans which pull up just outside the gate and exhume a number of large male bodies who briefly group together before splitting into two groups. The first two men make their way towards the guard, who has already stepped out of his box and waits for them to approach. After a few brief nods and a glance towards the vehicles he leads them towards the offices and through the main door. The other two start to unload equipment from the open doors of the first vehicle. They each wear almost identical black army trousers and grey sweatshirts over which there hangs a small rectangle of card on a long metal chain.

All the refugees are watching them closely now, curious to know the reason for this intrusion into their private ritual of grief. When the men have arranged five heavy metal cases on the ground, one of them heaves a camera onto his right shoulder while the other one picks up a box and reams of looping wire which drag behind him in the dirt. There is a quick stiffening of the nerves, an instinctual bristle of suspicion. Turning slowly, the cameraman films the waste area around the camp, then moves closer to pan in on the entrance and the guard box. Then the two of them move closer towards the office and are met by their colleagues accompanied by the director of the camp and the social worker. Again there is a soundless discussion, before the staff retreat and the camera crew approach the crowd.

'Ask her where she is from.'
'Otkuda Vy?' a voice translates into Russian but the woman in front of the microphone shakes her head and answers in her own

tongue, moving her body behind those which surround her in an attempt to escape.

'We are here to get your story out to the world; if you don't cooperate this war will be ignored and forgotten. We are here to give you a chance to tell your story!'

The voice is unmistakably Lithuanian but his Russian is almost perfect.

'These are the names of my both my sons,' a woman's hand thrusts itself forward waving two sheets of Red Cross paper and the camera searches for her face amongst the crowd.

'Ask her what they were doing there? Were they with the rebels?'

The voice translates obediently but the reply is obliterated by the rush of words which compete for airspace. There are other women now, desperately waving the thin sheets of paper and repeating names like a litany of the dead.

'When was the last time you managed to get a phone line home?'

'Who of you can speak Russian well?'

Heedlessly, the voices continue to call out the names of their relatives, while the foreigners try to shift position in order to get a better shot at the crowd. The camera scans the crowd again, then homes in on his face.

'Vy govorite po russki?'

'I can speak English also, if you want,' he answers flatly.

'Quick, over here!'

'What are these people queuing here for?'

'They wait to give the name of their family to the Red Cross. Then they will put them on a database and they will try to find them amongst the prisoners....the survivors.'

'Do you have family left behind?'

'My mother, my cousins.'

'Do you have any relatives in the terrorist forces?'

'Why do you call them terrorists? They also fight for what they think is right.'

He smarts as if he is struck and tries to move from the camera back into the mesh of bodies around him.

'Wait! What town do you come from?'

He turns back on them, seeking the eyes of the one who spoke to him amongst the unfamiliar faces.

The interviewer's eyes widen in interest as he articulates the name which has no longer seems to belong to his own past but to the legend of distant battles. Moving in closer, the reporter tries to intercept him with a thrust of the microphone, signalling to the cameraman to do the same.

'What was your reaction to the scenes which came through this morning? Did you expect a mass killing of that scale?'

'What are talking about?'

'The digging of the mass grave picked up by the spy cameras. The suspected termination of the remaining population?'

'Termination? What the fuck do you mean?'

The face of the journalist flinches and he waves the cameraman to step back. He is no longer surrounded by his own people but out on his own on the other side, in the territory of the foreigners.

'You didn't see the footage?'

From out of nowhere he is handed a handful of back and white photos. He reaches for them; his eyes desperately trying to focus on a familiar object. There is a dark area of bushiness and lines scored on the earth and then a wide, black void partially filled with soft organic forms which look to him like worms or moles. His mind cannot understand the scale of the images; if the lines are those made by a hoe or by a heavy vehicle; if the smeared dark patches are weeds or trees. It is only after a few seconds of looking that he realises the limp, bald shapes are human bodies and the rest of the objects suddenly jerk into perspective.

Somewhere in the folds of his mind, he is reminded of those other colourless photographs, portraying another massacre.

'You come here to show us this?'

He does not wait for an answer, moving forward with every muscle of his body.

'Who the hell are you to come here and put this in our faces?'

The journalist turns and falls backwards, colliding with his cameraman and contorting awkwardly from the ungainly weight of the other man pushing him towards the hard earth. Unexpectedly, his feet give way and his colleague falls wide of him; so that all he can do is tuck his head under the protection of his arms to shield him from the blows.

'Get him off!'
'Pomogite yemu!'
Through his shoes Azad can feel the flesh give and the form buckle away from his kicks. There are arms which try to encircle his, a grating feeling like gravel along his jaw line, but he is without feeling.
'Hold him back!'
'Call the police, somebody. What are you all staring at?'

After the longest time, he is finally free of pain and will not let go of the sensation of liberation. Time is stretched and smoothed into a place where there is only the power of his own limbs flexing and retracting, while his mind slips into the eternal bliss of un-thinking. Even when the air has been expelled from his lungs and his body jolts against the concrete, he is left with a white vastness of nothing expanding gently across his consciousness.

16

He had not planned to come to her house, yet when he finds himself nearing the streets of her quarter he is pleased with the appropriateness of it. As he walks, he is aware only of the dull ache in his left side every time his foot jars against the unrelenting concrete. He knows that his lip must also be damaged, because he can taste the rusty tang of blood whenever he runs his tongue along the uneven surface where the soft flesh borders with the rough stubble. Since the adrenalin has retreated from his bloodstream he has managed to maintain his breathing at a steady rate, although his heart is still leaping inside his ribcage. The compact form of the mobile phone lies comfortably in his pocket – hard and solid against the flesh of his leg.

As he approaches the door, he can see that the light in the kitchen is on, although there is no movement behind the shutter-less window. He knocks and is surprised at how hard his hand raps on the wood. From somewhere he has the sensation he is being watched but it lasts only a second before he hears a latch being a drawn back and the key turning in the lock.

Lucy winces involuntarily when she sees his face full on; it is not just the bruise on his lower cheek and the blood on his lip which shock her but the heavy darkness which rests around the eyes and seems to draw his features together in one taut configuration of suppressed panic.
'Can I come in?'
He does not wait for an answer, moving past her into the still-dishevelled kitchen space. Silently, he takes off his coat and rests it on the back of a chair. She is still staring at him, her mouth slightly open in an expression which annoys him.

'Haven't you got anything to say?'
Quickly, she lowers her eyes from his face.
'Do you want a coffee?'
He laughs dryly and looks around the cupboards which line the wall.
'Don't you have anything proper to drink?'
She falters, then bends down to open the fridge.
'Only this.'
Not knowing what to do with her hands, she thrusts the bottle towards him so that the clear liquid swishes inside but he doesn't reach out for it in return, so that for a few seconds she is left standing in a ridiculous pose. Hesitantly, she takes two glasses from the draining board and puts them down on the empty table. Her hands shake as she pours.
'I watched the news last night. I'm so sorry.'
His eyes flick to hers, then away again. Every gesture of his body tells her not to continue but she is not of his world: where she comes from everything must be voiced out-loud, discussed and analysed.
'Did you manage to talk to your family?'
'I got the news a few hours ago - I have no family anymore.'

The flatness of his voice makes her start and she looks away as he takes his glass and drinks back the vodka in one mouthful. Roughly, he takes the bottle and tips it towards him so that the liquid pours clumsily, spilling onto the wood and soaking into its grooves and knots.

Feeling her courage draining out of her, she leans over and brushes the back of her hand against his. He reaches for her and pulls her towards him, so that their faces are close enough to kiss. Caught under his gaze like an insect beneath a microscope, she resists the temptation to twist away. For the first time since entering he looks into her eyes and seems to find in them something which both entices and repels him. Only when she gasps from the pain in her arm where he holds her does he lose focus and let his hand fall gently across her front, brushing the side of her breast clumsily, then holding her so tight that she feels imprisoned. His kiss is dry and furious.

'I'm in love with you.'
He raises his hand towards her mouth in order to stop her, but comes short of touching it. His head is averted as if avoiding a blow.
'It could be different...' she continues, 'I could leave Benjamin. I would do that if...'
He would like to turn now and to look her directly in the eyes but his pride will not allow it.
'And what when you decide to go back home? What then?'
'I could stay here.'
'I have *temporary leave to remain*,' he pronounces the words as if he is reading them from his identity card, 'I stay here just as long as the government allows me. If they decide tomorrow that it is safe to go back to my country, they will force me to go.'
'But how can it be safe? That's out of the question now...'
'They only need a cease-fire, a promise...who cares what happens later.'
'But can't you stay? Isn't there a process where you can ask to stay on humanitarian grounds?' she searches in her mind for the right word, 'ask for asylum?'
'You are an expert now, I see.'
'We would both be just foreigners here then.'
'No, you are an ex-patriot and I would always be an immigrant. Try to understand, this is not about you and me. It has gone too far for that anymore.'
He takes his cigarettes from his shirt pocket and lights one. There is no stray gesture from his hands which would indicate the dreadful pressure of the blood pulsating in his veins.

'You told me you saw what happened last night. You didn't see anything.'

She does not dare to answer him; his bitterness is terrifying.

'How can you watch that and pretend to understand. This is not one moment - this is the last part of a story that is hundreds of years old – thousands of years old. A story of people pushed down, made to march for other armies, made to...' his English fails him and he raises his hands in the air and lets them drop to his sides. 'You cannot watch a thing like this on the TV and understand....'

He jerks his chin at her in a gesture which is both provocative and admonishing.

'When you watch those Muslims on the news channels, their faces full of anger, dancing around an American flag that someone puts on fire, do you think that is reality? Do you think that those men – in their village – can buy an American flag to put on fire? I cannot even buy an American flag here in Vilnius!'

He looks at her and she has the impression that he has already decided she won't understand, already relegated her to the status of foreigner.

'Everybody knows who your people are. Everybody watches the films, listens to the music. But we are unknown. We are hidden by our geography and by our history. If I tell you we are modern people who live without extremism and want only peace, you can believe me or you can look at those pictures of angry men shouting for revenge. But nobody sees people like me. They don't want to hear about our side: our pain, our hopes. I am invisible to the cameras.'

He takes up the glass again and moves into the living room, leaving her bereft of even his ambivalence. Inside her there are the stirrings of an old instinct; a desire to pursue things to the very end.

'I heard about the incident with the TV people.'

He rounds on her with a rekindling of anger, so that she stops short of approaching him.

'How do you know about that?'

'One of the crew told me.'

'Crew?'

'One of the guys who works on the team, he's a friend...an acquaintance of mine from college. He must have found out I was working here through our school internet site and he contacted me to ask for advice on places to visit. They were supposed to be doing a feature on Lithuania but then when this happened they were asked to do a news feature, a human interest program - reactions to the news among the refugee population.' She pauses for breath; she has been speaking too fast, 'no-one can get into your country, so this was the next best thing.'

'The next best thing,' his tone remains flat, so that she is unsure if he is mocking her. 'Do you know what they brought with them to show us? What pictures they had?'

'I didn't mean...'

'They brought photos of the massacre to share with us.'

He lets out a short, sharp exhalation of breath in an attempt at black humour. 'They – Lithuanians, Americans, everybody – have photos of our dead but we, the people who have family there, are not told what has happened. Our mothers and fathers and our sisters and brothers - we have to watch foreign photographs and television to know what happened to them. Some of the people in the centre, they only know their family is dead because they see the bodies on TV.'

She jars at the image his last comment creates in her mind, searching desperately for some way to defend herself,

'They came to interview you so that people can hear your side of the story.'

'That is just the problem' he retaliates, 'to you it is a story. Another story to listen to from your safe home with your big cars and your important jobs. We are not real people to the West, we are just obscure tribes who only know about war and corruption: rebels, terrorists. The West finds a cause to hate and supports any government who goes against it – even if that government is criminal. First they hate communism and now they hate Islam. So now everyone in my hometown is a Muslim fundamentalist!' She sighs, then lowers her voice to a whisper, 'It's not us against you.'

'Isn't it? Do you give us any other choice with your propaganda and your pre-emptive attacks? Look what you have done to Afghanistan, to Iraq…'

She makes as if to move towards him, but he raises his hand to stop her. Behind each of his words lie the dreadful force of fury and desperation.

'You should not have told them to come to the refugee centre. It's the only place we have left.'

'I'm sorry. I thought it might do some good.'

'Good?' And in your country you know all about that: about what is good for everybody else.'

'I am not America or the West. Why are you talking to me as if you hated me?'

He lets his eyes search her body as if he is seeing her for the first time; slowly following the lines of her figure then resting back on her face. In her expression he notices an unbearable mixture of desire and pity.

He approaches her as she stands, her back against the wardrobe. Indistinctly, she hears him say something in which she catches only the words 'hate' and 'need'. There is no resistance in her body now; she is like liquid pouring over him. Taking the front of her blouse, he pulls at the soft material so that it rips but she makes only the faintest of sighs. It is not until he has entered her that she lets out the cry she must have been suppressing. He is aware of the rough wood at her back, the tightness of his hands on her arms, but refuses to look into her eyes or to touch her lips. His face is close to her chest, near the veins which spider like blue threads under the paper-thin skin, so much paler against the contrast of his. Her bones seem to have acquired the fragility of bird's wings under the thin layer of flesh and momentarily he is spellbound with the thought that he could break them with the minimum of effort. It is not until he has let her go, feeling her body buckle and fall back against the sofa, that he allows himself to look at her face: stained with the effort of pain and relief.

He gets up and fastens his trousers, pulling the belt tight then letting his shirt fall loosely over it; the pale light from the window silhouetting his slow deliberate movements. She can hear the quickness of his breath matching hers, as if they were still linked together. Passing near the place where she fell, for one moment she has the impression that he will turn and speak to her but it is only the slightest of hesitations in his walk and a few seconds later she hears the door open and close. Senselessly, her hand moves to pull the torn material across her breasts.

***

There is only time for the phone to ring once, before the click of connection and a male voice answering abruptly in a language which he does not recognise, then immediately switching to English in the split second it takes him to catch his breath.
'You must be in the main train station at 21:00'
'How will I know you?'
'We will find you.'
The line is cut and he is left staring at the small, rectangular screen as the light from it pales and dies. Cautiously, he locks the keyboard and slips the phone back into his trouser pocket – already it has left a sore patch on his thigh where it swings as he walks and presses against him when he is seated.

There are beads of perspiration on his upper lip despite the chill in the air and he wipes them away with the back of his coat sleeve. It is already late afternoon and the winter light is muted and mild. Somehow he has ended up in a small park between tall, concrete buildings; a pale strip of grass which has been worn to a few torn patches of dirty green by the passers-by and the wheels of the cars which mount the pavement and infringe on its borders. It must once have been a place that was used by local mothers and children, for there are still the carcasses of an old swing and a rusted climbing frame; their bright red colour still visible in patches.

Sitting on the back of the only bench, he lets his feet rest on the one plank that remains of the seat. There is nobody near him, nobody who would have noticed his hurried call or the way he stuffed the phone back into his pocket like someone getting rid of a soiled handkerchief. The only other human beings around are a pair of middle-aged women propped against the side of a far building, their shopping bags dropped temporarily at their feet as they talk in loud voices. They do not notice him, bound as they are in their impenetrable world of schools and washing, groceries and the endless preparation of food. He glances as them briefly and then swallows down the memories of his own family, which rise up from inside of him like bile.

Somewhere in the distance he hears a siren and automatically his body flinches. Already the feeling of suspicion has settled on his skin, so that nothing around him is neutral anymore. He is acutely aware that by making that one short call he has implicated himself in something which is larger than him or the sum of all he has been until now.

Slowly, he lets his hand slide into his pocket and pull out the phone again. He allows a few minutes to slip by as his eyes rest on it, then unlocks the keyboard and begins to dial a number. He expects (perhaps even hopes) that the line to the centre will be busy but the dial tone rings through and a child's voice answers.

'Can I speak to Benjamin, room A6.'

There is a scuffle of activity and the receiver is placed heavily on the desk. He can count in his head the number of steps it takes to reach his barrack and find the right door; the seconds it takes for Benjamin to stop what he is doing and put on his shoes and coat, before making his way out to the phone room.

'Hello?'

Strangely, he finds himself unprepared for the conversation and his voice will not respond.

'Hello? Is there anybody there?'

'It's me.'

Sharply, Benjamin's voice drops to a whisper. 'Where the hell are you?'

'In town.'

'They called the police, they were here for some time but the guy didn't want to press charges.'

'I want you to give Zahra a message.'

'What are you talking about?'

'Just tell her something from me.'

'Tell her yourself. There's no reason not to come back, it was a normal reaction, none of us knew what...'

'You're not listening.'

Benjamin stops himself – it is so quiet at the other end of the line it seems that the connection must have been cut. 'Are you still there?'

'Just tell her that she has to be proud.'

'Proud of what?'

Azad laughs tersely and ignores the comment, as if he is talking only to himself. 'That she should see this as a gesture for her, for all of us. Tell her that this is my wedding gift.'

He cuts the line before Benjamin has had a chance to answer: he does not want to allow any of them the chance to dissuade him from what he has to do. Stepping down from the seat, he closes his coat against the evening's chill. Nearby, a clock chimes five and the two women stir as if from an involuntary sleep and start to move towards their homes and their briefly forgotten routines. Moving very close to them as he exits between the buildings, he notices the expensive perfume draped over the cheap clothes, before the odour of exhaust again takes over again and he is back on the main road.

17

The station is a large and hollow place; the low ceiling of its main hall seeming to crush the last remnants of fresh air out through the narrow exits so that the atmosphere is cold and stale. He is one of only a handful of human forms scattered across the empty marble space like birds wandering the pavement. Above them, the black information board hangs static over their heads; its contents reduced to four last destinations. He reads the names out silently to himself: two local trains to towns he has never heard of and two internationals bound for Moscow and Berlin. The prospect of going east causes a reaction inside him which is a mixture between dread and excitement. It is an uneasy concoction of knowledge and memory – a recalling of his happiness as a boy when he would return home after summers with Alma and the realisation that he would no longer be welcome in the place which was once the heart of the empire.

He scans the hall again for a sign of the person who will meet him; searching for a face which will look his way, for the nod of the head or some signal that he must follow. There are two men huddled together near the ticket counter whose paleness and flimsy suits classify them as Easterners, while to his left there is a young Lithuanian couple saying goodbye to each other. He notices the reticence in the girl's body as she moves towards the platform while her boyfriend looks after her, then turns to light a cigarette and walks away towards the exit. The other figures are less distinct: two young men with coloured backpacks whom he dismisses as tourists and an elderly man laying in a drunken sprawl on one of the benches.

He checks his watch - it is nine fifteen. Almost immediately there is a brief vibration from the phone in his pocket. The message comes from an unknown number and contains three words: toilets - first cubicle. Cautiously, he clears the screen and walks to the door which is indicated between two locked kiosks selling magazines and sweets. Checking for the attendant, he jumps across the pay barrier and enters into the tiled room, his nostrils instantly smarting from the sharp odour of urine which assails him. Unexpectedly, he does not find someone waiting for him; only two vacant cubicles, their doors swung open.

Despite the emptiness around him, he looks over his shoulder before stepping inside and closing the door. Disappointingly, the interior contains only the usual smeared tiles and the childish graffiti; no sign of the thing he is expected to find. Stepping up onto the toilet seat he runs his hands along the top of the cistern and feels a thin slice of paper move beneath his fingers. He takes it down quickly and tears open the seal of the brown envelope which he has retrieved. Inside there is a second-class ticket to Berlin, five hundred Euro and a Lithuanian passport. His hands are shaking so much that he barely manages to put the items into his pocket and he hesitates before throwing away the envelope.

When he steps out again into the station foyer, he straightens himself and walks calmly to the platform, conscious all the while of the hidden eyes which must be watching him. He will not allow himself to falter; he must get on the train and take his place as if it were the most natural thing he had ever done. He does not know if it is a desperate confidence in those who are leading him, or the cold anger inside him which allows him to continue walking despite the fear which has crept down into his legs and threatens to make him stumble. He checks the eyes of a female passenger whom he passes outside the carriages but cannot notice anything in her expression which would indicate that his fear is visible.

Only when the carriage doors have been shut and the train has begun shunting out of the station does he take the passport out of his pocket and search for the details of his new identity. The covers are still stiff and shiny and yet not new enough to provoke undue suspicion. Inside, he finds his photograph sealed perfectly behind the laminated plastic with the name Andrius Savukynas. He runs his thumb over the data, desperately searching his mind for an explanation as to how they could have obtained his picture without his knowledge. It is an exact copy of the one he had taken for his university identity badge – and now he holds the two of them together to compare. The sudden memory of the librarian at his department makes him pause; the so familiar features, the underlying feeling of recognition which always lingered between them. An unexpected chill ripples across his skin at the thought that his world was more porous than he could have imagined. Hurriedly, he folds the stiff plastic of his ID card in half and tries to break it by folding it back and forth. When it finally gives, he opens the window just enough to let the document slip down onto the tracks, then closes it immediately and sits back down.

Perhaps it is the gentle rocking of the train, or perhaps it is simply delayed exhaustion, but no sooner have the lights of the city receded than he is slumped into a dreamless slumber. His trance is broken at one o'clock by the screeching of the brakes and a rush of movement which swells along the corridors. Abruptly, his door is swung open and from behind the drawn curtain he faces a man in uniform.
'Lithuanian customs control.'
Leaning forward, he hands his new passport to the outstretched hand which waits for him, then sits back in his place. He can see

his own reflection in the darkened glass and notices the tension in the pursed lips and the corner of his eyes. He hopes that the bruise on his jaw-line will not be noticeable beneath the dark stubble which has begun to cover his chin.

'Where are you travelling to?'

'To Berlin.'

He doesn't offer any further explanation, hoping that he has managed to camouflage his accent in these two hastily spoken words. The guard looks up at the empty racks above his head and frowns, then moves down the corridor. He can hear the other doors being opened and the low mumble of words being spoken from a distance. The inside of the cabin is cold and yet he can feel his skin become damp as he swallows the fear back inside himself.

The train remains stationary for what seems to be the longest time but he doesn't dare to go into the corridor and show himself through the wide glass windows. Outside, there is only the creak and grunt of the metal breathing and the bright lights of the border post shining through the thin fabric of the curtains. Gradually the noise of human movement starts up again and he can hear the Polish customs officials making their way towards him.

The two guards that arrive are very young and they stand close together as if reassured by the sense of unity. One of them holds out his hand to receive the passport and proceeds to turn each page carefully while his colleague shuffles into the compartment and runs his eyes around the surfaces and the racks above. With an unexpected gesture of violence, he kicks the casing underneath the opposite seat, then does the same to the other side; checking for illegal goods or concealed bodies.

'Savukynas?'

'Da,' he answers a little too quickly, his mind already poised for the moment to pounce.

'Where are you going?'

The guard speaks in English, causing him to hesitate at little before he finds the right words.

'To Germany.'

'For what purpose?'

'To visit friends.'

The passport is still in the guard's hands, open at the details of his assumed identity.

'Do you have any money with you?'

His hand moves to retrieve his wallet, where he knows the crisp new Euro notes lay folded.

'Ok, ok,' the guard dismisses the gesture and takes a stamp from his uniform pocket, bringing it down noisily on an empty page of the document, then handing it over. The two of them exchange a brief glance and then they are gone in a trail of receding noises.

There is an extended silence which seems to stretch itself along the corridor like a passing breeze and then the wheels shift the weight of the vehicle into motion. For the first time in his life, he feels his own lack of religion like a handicap which inhibits movement. His ex-girlfriend had once said that communism was a disease which had eaten away their souls, so that there was nothing left for a person to rely on but man and his inevitable corruption.

He leans his head against the too-cold glass and tries to focus his gaze away from his own reflection and onto the vague shapes which can be glimpsed in the darkness. The train rumbles on, cutting through the heart of things: parting roads and parks and slipping noisily past empty gardens. In the night scene outside the window everything is reduced to monochrome: a street lamp illuminating the wet tarmac, the light from a living room accentuating the shadows which move behind the glass, a white cat silhouetted by the glow from the carriages.

Beneath his ribcage the pain of his fall still throbs and instinctively he lifts his hand to his face, touching the outline of his lips and letting his fingers put the slightest of pressure on the bruised cheek. The muscles in his arms and legs ache as if from sustained physical effort, but he knows it is only the attempt to hold himself together which has exhausted them. Every inch of his flesh longs for sleep and yet his mind will not give up its hold on consciousness. Now that he is awake, he is afraid of letting himself slip into that unprotected state of sleep where he cannot guard against the betrayal of sentiment. He tries hard to concentrate on the hunger in his belly, which keeps him chained to the physical. Only once during his vigil did his eyes slide close for a few seconds and immediately there were the twisted human forms rising up at him from the glossy photographic paper.

***

It is past midday by the time he reaches Berlin, and he steps nervously out of the train like an animal let loose from its cage after a long time. He cannot get rid of the feeling that the rage inside him has somehow seeped into his skin, so that his very flesh gives off the stench of hostility. Hanging back until he is alone on the platform, he walks slowly into the main building.

The shops in the station have already brought out the paraphernalia of commercial Christmas cheer: the coloured lights looped around the window fronts, stencils of reindeer and snow flakes speckling the cold glass, tinny music regurgitating the festive message. Stopping to light a cigarette, he catches a glimpse of his reflection in the plate glass of a store: the creased clothes and the darkly circled eyes peering out above the black stubble on his chin. For one second, he is caught by the familiarity of the features without even recognising himself. Stubbing out the cigarette and entering one of the shops, he purchases a disposable razor and shaving cream and with the change he pays for one of the toilet cubicles. He is not tempted to buy any of the pre-packaged food on offer, for he is beginning to find a kind of purity in his hunger which is addictive. Now that his bodily functions have been reduced to a minimum, his only focus is on the task ahead of him.

Once he has shaved and washed his face and neck, he sits down on one of the numerous metal benches and waits to be contacted. On the far wall, he can see the long list of destinations changing and rearranging as trains leave and arrive: Hamburg; Antwerp; Amsterdam; Paris. He takes out the mobile phone and lets it rest lightly in the palm of his hand. Sitting with his body tense and his breath shallow, he does not allow himself to open up the Pandora's Box of his conscience. Perversely, he will not even listen to that small, fading voice of reason which has accompanied him all these years, for gushing over the top of it there comes an almost forgotten sense of satisfaction.

He does not have to wait long before he feels the vibration of an incoming message. The instructions tell him to purchase an onward ticket to Geneva, and to leave on the three-thirty train. Immediately, he takes the precaution of deleting the communication and puts the phone safely back in his pocket. There is a perfect simplicity in these bleeps of information which come to him from nowhere and return to nowhere, an almost mathematical purity which pleases him. He can derive a sense of calmness from the faceless efficiency which now leads him forward: after so many months of inertia, it feels like liberation.

18

Despite the tough secularism of his mind, he is struck by the sense of destiny which overwhelms him when the train passes the German/Swiss border without stopping for customs control. Wryly, he thinks how this innate belief in fate is not something which could ever have been erased by socialist theory or the sensory bribery of capitalism – it is something which every one of his compatriots is born with.

Suddenly he is overwhelmed with the idea that the world is full of such signs and wonders, if only he could be open to the subtlety of their messages. His head is full of messages and half-finished conversations: urgent admonitions, soft reproaches, the high–pitched voice of accusation gouging out a hollow inside him. He slips in and out of a shallow sleep while the wheels beneath him slide across the rails with a soft and regular rumble.

All along his slow journey there are designated places where he has to change trains: Mannheim, Basel, Olten, Biel: interruptions slicing through his night and hindering any attempt at rest. It is early morning when the train starts to slow down to enter Geneva; the sun steadily rising to illuminate a milky skyline opening out onto a vast expanse of pale water. His eyes rest gratefully on the pallid hues as the lake ripples and undulates beneath the gentle light, giving him the sensation of weightlessness. For a few minutes his mind empties itself of all thoughts, leaving nothing but the synthesis of the elements and the gentle forward motion pulling him onwards.

When the engine finally cuts, he watches the other passengers file past and push towards the exit. Observing their expensive clothes and shoes he is shocked by the profound sense of repulsion which unexpectedly wells up inside him. Superimposed across every neat and groomed face he can see the emaciated features of his countrymen being led out of the bunker; the effect is so real that he can almost smell the putrid odour of fear. Only when there is no more danger of physical contact does he get up from his seat and make his way to the platform.

The wind outside still carries the bitter cold of the night in it, making him shiver as the icy air enters his lungs and causing him to lose his step. His lack of food over the past two days have heightened his consciousness but weakened his body, so that he has to lean against a railing for a few seconds before he regains his balance.

The sound of the phone ringing is at once alien and completely expected, and he takes it from his pocket with a feigned nonchalance.
'Hello?'
'You do not need to answer, just listen: at nine o'clock you must wait on one of the benches in the Park des Cropettes. A man will sit beside you but you must not speak to him. When he gets up, he will leave a bag behind. The instructions will be in the front pocket.'

Even though the line has gone dead, he keeps the phone resting in his hand. There are the mumblings of yearning inside him, the voice of an instinct which he has been trying so hard to ignore. Impulsively, his fingers begin to punch in the numbers he knows so well, the numbers which will connect him to the only home he now possesses. Despite himself, there is even some glint of hope which is still illuminated in his mind. Again, it is the sense of a greater destiny which leads him, the surrender to a belief that fate will ultimately dictate each step of the journey. And so it is with the hard drop of inevitability that he hears a voice speak back at him – the stiffness of digitally created tones telling him that there are insufficient funds on his account to make the call.

He puts the phone away and searches along the wall for a city map or some plan of the area. Finding one near the east exit of the station, he easily orientates himself by the long sweep of the railway tracks cutting downwards from the north and the wide blue stretch of the lake. He finds the park immediately behind the station: a small rhomboid of green criss-crossed by pathways.

Taking the stairs to street level, he comes out at the back of the building and crosses a small road which leads him to the entrance of the park. Not knowing which way to turn, he follows the central gravel path and walks towards the encompassing green of the grass and trees. In a small clearing, he sits down on an empty bench placed near a drinking fountain. Around him, there is still the morning bustle of workers walking to their jobs, carrying plastic cups of take-away coffee and heavy bags slung across their shoulders. He looks at each one carefully, trying to distinguish in them the potential for violence. His hands rest uselessly in his lap and he regrets not buying a newspaper, even if he would not understand the words written there.

He does not know how long he has been waiting, when a young man in jogging gear brushes very close to his leg and sits down beside him. Resisting the urge to turn and stare, he can nevertheless make out the unexpected Aryan features; the blue eyes and the short blond hair. The man puts down his rucksack on the seat and bends forward in order to re-tie his shoelace. For a second it seems as if the whole episode is just a coincidence, but when the man gets up to leave he does not retrieve the bag from the bench.

His neck and back are damp from sweat as he gets to his feet and lifts the bag onto his shoulders. It is surprisingly heavy, and he falters a little from the weight of it. He knows that he must find a private place where he can sit and examine its contents in peace, and heads towards the café building which he can see on the edge of the park. Entering, he orders a coffee at the bar and asks for the key to the toilet.

Once inside, he locks the door behind him, then carefully lifts the bag from his shoulders and rests it on the sink. Undoing the zip of the front pocket, he pulls out a padded envelope and breaks open the seal. Inside, there are a number of items each packed in a separate plastic wallet. He opens the first one to find a map of the city marked with arrows and circles in thick red pen along with five colour photos of a glass and brick building. Reading the long line of blue lettering which wraps itself around the white curved entrance, he experiences a shallow undulation of satisfaction within him in the place where shock should be: United Nations High Commissioner for Refugees.

Examining the map closer, he traces with his finger the short walk indicated to arrive at the building. The logistics have been worked out perfectly; there is but five minutes between him and his target. Putting the map carefully into his coat pocket, he takes the photos and tears them into small pieces above the toilet basin, before flushing the chain noisily. He knows that the details have imprinted themselves onto his memory so securely that nothing will be able to erase them. He wonders with an almost clinical curiosity if these will be the last pictures he will see; if only he could rid himself of those other images which flicker constantly across his retina, then all of this might be different.

His heartbeat is so loud that it seems to fill his head, yet his hands remain steady as they extract a folded sheet of printed paper and a small plastic badge from the other two wallets. For the second time, he is taken aback by his own features staring out at him above the now familiar name: Andrius Savukynas, Economist, Division of Financial and Administrative Management, UNHCR. He turns it over in his hand, at once horrified and enthralled by the perfection of it.

Gently unhooking the clasp on the front of the rucksack, he peers inside at the two containers of clear liquid linked by adhesive tape and wires; they have been packed carefully in insulating material like precious canisters of wine prepared for a picnic. His year in the military service has given him some experience of explosives and the starting mechanism is familiar to him. The device is a simple one, an amateur attempt at causing the maximum devastation with the minimum of sophistication.

Stopping at the bar, he drinks back the coffee and smarts at its bitterness. It is the first thing to enter his stomach in a long while and he feels the muscles spasm in shock. Behind the rows of half-empty bottles lined against the wall he can just make out his own reflection in the mirror, and starts at shocking reproduction of his mother's features he sees reflected there. The unexpected memory makes him flinch, before his mind realigns and immediately starts to consider the task before him like he would a mechanical problem. He understands very well that the chances of getting past the UN security guards without a bag search would be almost nil, despite the identity badge, and yet his mind has been steeling itself to this scenario from the first moment he retrieved the phone from under the mattress. He does not want a way back into a world which no longer contains any tenderness.

He knows that an explosion anywhere inside the building will cause the devastation that he is aiming for. It is up to him now to bring the reality of the war into this neat, smug little country; to show these complacent people what it is like to have reality crash down around them. Horror is no longer the reserve of the third world – it can be brought right into the heart of so-called civilisation.

***

The avenue which leads to the tall, glass building is lined with high flag poles. Sheets of coloured fabric flap frantically above his head and in vain he searches for the emblem of his fledgling nation. He has already decided that this will not be the moment: this is the reconnaissance, his way of preparing himself for what must be. Each footstep he takes now will be repeated later with dull finality.

He can already see the tell-tale sign of the UN building from far away. Not daring to come too near the guarded entrance, he hangs back and lights a cigarette. From where he is standing he can see the guards clustered near the doorway and the marble flooring beyond which he cannot allow his imagination to wander. The faces of the men are hard and immobile, like masks which they don each morning and leave behind when they go home. For him, they are simply the uniforms and the policy of exclusion; he can see no humanity in their authoritarian poses and he notices a sense of satisfaction rise up inside him at how easily he has managed to remove himself from the personal. With a long-practised gesture, he throws away the cigarette butt and grinds it into the concrete.

He is almost home and dry, almost liberated, when he notices a woman approaching him: burnished skin, auburn hair. Her face does not reveal beauty but some rare strain of kindness which he has not seen for a long time. For one brief moment he is caught in her vision, so that it seems to be him who is the object of her gaze. Mirrored across time and space, it takes him a split second to comprehend, and turning his head he finds the object of her love: a small girl of about five years old running to embrace her. Immediately, he averts his gaze as if he has intruded on an intimacy not meant for outside eyes. His skin bristles with the sudden, almost tangible sensation of lewdness and he is overwhelmed by the idea that his clothes are impregnated with the dirt and sweat of the past few days and that the stink of them has become overpowering.

Without thinking, he starts to pull at his collar as if he would tear the cloth. For a few blind seconds, he has the uncontrollable desire to scratch away even the first layer of skin in an attempt to cleanse himself of the filth which has seeped into him. His breath struggles to regain order over his body and the panic passes as quickly as it arrived. There is only the slightest twitch of his head, as if he trying to throw off an unwanted thought that has gate-crashed his mind, and then he is walking again.

His legs urge him forward as if to run, so that he has to consciously control their rhythm. He has no internal plan of where he will go, and yet some inner force directs him away from the concrete and the people towards the shimmering blue of the water he can just make out in the distance. It is like the recollection of something beautiful which he once possessed and yearns to own again.

He searches his memory for anything which resembles a prayer; some rhythmic talisman to protect his consciousness from the doubt which is seeping in through the crevices. Out on the lake, there are distant white smudges of movement as sailboats cruise across its agitated surface.

'A lone white sail shows for an instant,
Where gleams the sea, an azure streak...

Suddenly he can hear the Russian words enter his consciousness; the lilts of swooping vowels and the tight knots of consonants, and he scrambles for the lyrics which lie like abandoned toys across his childhood memory.

What left it in its homeland distant?
In alien parts what does it seek?

....And yet for storm it begs, the rebel,
As if in storm lurked calm and peace!'

He repeats the last eight words over and over in his head, finding in them a mantra that he can wrap himself inside. He needs words now like a hungry man needs food; they are the weapons with which he can protect himself from the thoughts that attack. These thoughts of his are dangerous - they find their forms in the images which lie neglected in his sub-conscious. The recollection of a face, the stray intonation of a voice calling through the air and he could be felled.

As if in storm lurked calm and peace

As if in storm lurked calm and peace

He is a child again, lost in the back streets of his hometown, with the only point of reference the agitated voice of his mother calling to him from the doorway of their house - he is sitting at his desk in school, with the midday sun bearing down on him through the high, open windows – there is a girl whose mother was killed in a car crash – small, perfectly round tears fall slowly down her cheeks as the teacher continues his explanation - a map which is pinned to the wall of their classroom, on which the United Kingdom appears coloured a fleshy pink – do you know why it is always pink? – to represent all the blood that was spilled in its name – blood, bright red and bitter as rust, sucked from the wound on his lip that he made while shaving with his first razor in front of the bathroom mirror - he can see his face reflected in the glass which has started to peel away in silver slivers around the bevelled edges – the smooth skin flushed in patches with the almost unbearable self-consciousness of puberty, his green eyes fading into brown around the rim of the iris: the black pinpoint of the entry to his self, the self that he tried so desperately to find, standing in front of the glass and staring, staring at what some might call the soul, the essence of this person which he has carried around inside his skin since before he knew how to remember - he can almost feel that he has reached it now, that he is standing on the very brink of meaning – there is wind on his face from the rushing of souls to meet his, he knows with absolute clarity those that will survive and those which will fall – they face him now in two equal lines, the doomed and the saved amid the constant drum of the falling grenades - the streets of his town crumbling like bread between the fingers, rupturing and gushing inside-out on the pavements and the grass verge and the roadside, covering the cracks between the paving stones which he would so carefully avoid as he returned from school – step, jump, step, jump.....thirty four, thirty five, thirty six, until he reached the stone stairs and past the door of the woman whose husband was arrested in the middle of the night, with only a thud on the floorboards and the whine of suppressed screams through the plaster and the wood - in the blue stillness of a perfect sky he can see the neck and shoulders of the girl with whom he lost his virginity; can feel the contraction of the climax; see the stain of blood on the worn, yellow sheets - his whole vision is filled with blood now: the red of heavy wine and poppies in the afternoon sun – the red of the organs which spew from the torn flesh of the bodies which lie abandoned after the grenades have fallen, the thin trails of blood which trickle out of orifices after the bullets have struck - there is so much blood on the earth of his country that the soil will no longer pulsate with the life of the plants which have always grown there – it is no longer the blood of last week or today but the stains of hundreds of years which have seeped into the very rock – the rock which is the only thing that cannot be destroyed, which will survive when all the rest has been swept away by the wrath of god – the god who has lain for so long beneath the soil, like a hibernating creature ready to throw the sleep from its body when the spring returns – the god in whom he cannot believe and yet who leads him now into the calm heart of the storm............

DEATH BY FIRE LEAVES GENEVA STUNNED

The usually calm and affluent city of Geneva was shaken today after witnessing an unprecedented act of public violence when an unknown man set alight to himself in front of the main offices of the United Nations High Commissioner for Refugees.

The incident occurred just after lunch time in the business district of the city. Film taken from local security cameras shows a young man of Asian features dousing himself with liquid taken from a plastic bag, then igniting a lighter which sent a wall of flames shooting up his body. Traumatised eye-witnesses claim the man acted so fast that on-lookers were too shocked to react.

It is uncertain as to whether the identity of the man can be ascertained as his remains were charred beyond recognition. However, police have retrieved a suicide note found in the jacket that they believe he discarded just before his final act. Although the actual wording of the letter has not been made public, it has been indicated that the man was a refugee from Central Asia and was protesting against the on-going conflict in this region, which has cost thousands of lives over the past two years.

According to an eye-witness report the same man, aged somewhere in his mid-twenties, had been spotted earlier in the day in the same vicinity carrying a blue rucksack which another witness claims she saw him throw into the lake shortly after noon. As no such bag has been retrieved from the shoreline, the significance of its contents cannot be determined.

Speaking later this afternoon at a hastily-called news conference, the UNHCR spokesperson expressed her deep sadness at such an act of self-violence, but added that it served as a horrific reminder of the suffering which induces people to flee their homeland and seek safety in another country. She stated that the majority of the world's ten million refugees escape from conflicts which put themselves and their families in grave danger.

This evening in the peaceful city of Geneva, the story which lies behind the unknown man's act of desperation remains a mystery. Yet his self-immolation has already been hailed by some as the ultimate political gesture – the only form of protest powerful enough to drive home a plea for help which would otherwise be left unheard. An anonymous announcement claiming to be from an International Islamic organisation has appeared on unofficial Central Asian websites calling the suicide 'the supreme sacrifice' and 'the greatest act of love'.

1349005

Made in the USA